BECOMING NAVI

A NOVELLA ABOUT CHILD TRAFFICKING

SANDY STORM

Footprint Publishing
PO Box 1022
Roanoke, TX 76262
footprintpub.com

Quantity sales ordering information:

Special discounts are available on quantity purchases by survivors, associations, ministries and others. For details, please contact publisher at footprintpub.com.

Cover art and all images within this book created by artist Alexis Kadonsky. Learn more about her and her work at alexiskadonsky.com.

Footprint Publishing
~ leave an impression ~

For every child who has ever suffered sexual abuse.

CONTENTS

FOREWORD
BY: CATHY L. MILLER RN, PHD, CLNC

Associate Professor of Nursing at Texas A&M
University-Corpus Christi
Co-Chair Texas Costal Bend Border Region
Human Trafficking Task Force
Healthcare Consultant for Shared Hope
International
Technical Working Group Member and Trainer for
The United States Department of Health and
Human Services Office of Trafficking in Persons
Administration for Children and Families
National Human Trafficking Training and
Assistance Center-SOAR Program

Contact: cathy.miller@tamucc.edu

"We are all tied together in the single garment of destiny."

– DR. MARTIN LUTHER KING, JR.

Have you ever met a person, and then kept meeting that same person in various locations and venues across different geographic areas? If so, then like me, you must have felt a sense of fate, destiny, or a sense that God had a purpose for linking each of you. This divine intervention is how I came to be introduced to Sandy Storm.

I was presenting at the 2015 Shared Hope International JuST conference. After my presentation two lovely ladies approached me and introduced themselves, and all three of us were shocked that we were from the same South Texas town, and yet here we were at this conference in Washington, DC. All three on the same missions - to teach, learn, act, and eradicate child sex trafficking. I was asked to become involved in their outreach and victim services efforts and to help form our local anti-human trafficking task force. At the first meeting, I met Sandy, and then, it seemed everywhere I presented, trained, or attended meetings, Sandy was there. Her light, beauty, and absolute conviction drew me, and since then, we have been tied together through friendship, work, and our advocacy for human trafficking victims and survivors.

I had read and was deeply moved by *Hello Navi*, Sandy's first novella, so when she invited me to write the foreword for *Becoming Navi* I was, of course, humbled and honored. Then I was intimidated. How could I do justice to the intimate shared experiences of Navi? Then, He told me what to do, "Write from your heart."

As an Emergency Department nurse for over 20 years, almost 20 years ago I had my first experience with a child sex trafficking victim. Without going into the details, I would like to share that the little girl I cared for that night changed my life and career forever. I knew that God had brought that little one to ME - in my ER - that night for a reason, not only to provide her care, but to step up and change how health care providers and healthcare systems recognized, provided care, and referred child sex trafficking victims. We were failing miserably.

The crime of child sex trafficking is like a Pandora's box for the soul. Once someone is exposed to the mental and physical abuses endured by trafficking victims, one cannot walk away, ignore, or live in denial. The more we learn about child sex trafficking, the more difficult it is to understand how this crime continues. Even more difficult to understand is how victims and survivors pull resilience from the depths of their hearts and souls. For Sandy (*Navi*), it was her complete faith in God, and herself.

In my 20 years of working with, researching with, providing care for, and most importantly, learning from victims of human trafficking, one concept is consistent: Every person's story is different and every person's experiences are different. The end result of victimization by traffickers may be consistent, but the maze of different experiences and roads that led to their victimization are intensely personal and intimate.

Becoming Navi allows the reader the privilege of a very intimate view of one survivor's experience from a beginning filled with all the hopes, dreams, and unconditional love that is inherent in childhood, and shows how that love and desire to be loved in return can be abused and distorted.

After reading *Becoming Navi* you will be woven into our single garment of destiny. The mutual destiny of ending child sex trafficking. Wake up, stand up, and work to end child sex trafficking and provide support for the victims and survivors.

A word of caution as you read *Becoming Navi*: if you, dear reader, are a survivor of any type of abuse, for victims and survivors or any type of abuse, immersing oneself in anti-trafficking advocacy can be triggering, draining, and most of all, heart-wrenching. Trust me, I know. If you are not a survivor, listen to the words of Navi, and really let your heart hear. Then, make a plan to do something - anything within your community - to make a difference.

BECOMING NAVI

Some lay their sleepy heads,
At this time of day;
Others awaken as the cool breezes blow;
Ready to hunt, WILDLY

[1]
OUT OF THE DARKNESS

UTTER DARKNESS.

Not a sliver of light.

Not a flicker.

It would be a place of fear, but there was no fear.

It would be a place of despair, but that didn't exist there either.

It was just dark. And empty.

In that emptiness was a promise. In that darkness a promise of life glimmered.

Navi was there, in the darkness. She was hidden in the promise. She didn't know where she was and she didn't know about the promise. She didn't even know about the darkness, because darkness was all she had ever known.

Navi was absolutely still in the midst of the darkness, staying fixed and motionless. She didn't breathe or blink, she merely existed. She didn't know how long she had been there or what would happen next. The minutes passed like hours and the hours passed like days.

All at once, from out of nowhere, Navi felt a jolt as her world of darkness started to spin out of control. She was reeling and spinning in circles, whirling round and round and round. She opened her lungs for air and she opened her eyes but could see only the darkness. And in the darkness she heard a sound.

The sound was her father's voice. She could hear him yelling, screaming really. He was roaring with anger and violently screeching at the top of his lungs. The words he spouted were harsh and filthy, and he used a nasty tone that verified his rage.

Navi felt her heart begin to race. It beat so rapidly that it sounded like an army of horses rushing forth. Ba-bum, ba-bum, ba-bum, ba-bum, her heart pounded wildly. She continued spinning as her heart thumped.

The words were nearly audible and she could pick up on every other one or so. She knew her father was angry, and she knew her mother was crying. Maybe her father was hitting her mother, but she wasn't quite sure. In the darkness she strained to decipher the shouts.

"I'll cut it out of your belly if you won't go to the clinic!" her father barked. She heard her mother wailing and begging him to stop.

A loud crack was heard and suddenly Navi started spinning again. She went around three times and the rotations stopped just as quickly as they had started. She curled herself up into a ball and stuck her thumb into her mouth.

The darkness fell around her and she allowed it to envelop her once again.

She was safe and warm in that darkness. It was as if she had all she would ever need there. And best of all, she was hidden in the darkness. She was protected by that black, inky cloak. She wore the darkness as a covering. She received and accepted the darkness as a defining part of her identity.

As the days drug into weeks and the weeks drug on, Navi continued to hear the ramblings of her angry father and the wailings and moanings of her distraught mother. Every time, Navi would push herself further into the warmth of the dark cloak. It didn't matter who was right or who was wrong, she just wanted to hide. She felt abandoned, rejected and completely forsaken, left in the darkness with no one concerned about her at all.

Navi would sometimes ponder what life would be like outside of the darkness. All she knew of it was the fighting, the shouting, the smashing and the crying.

Although those were the sounds she had heard and the emotions she had experienced, there was a tiny flickering promise in her that caused her to dream. She would imagine life in wide open spaces, with light all around her. When her mind would take her to those beautiful places she would see a man with her - a strong father with square shoulders and a confidence about him that set her completely at ease.

Navi longed to be in the bright, open places with that father. When she was with him, the air smelled fresh and clean, not bloody and earthy like the darkness she was surrounded by. There was such a sharp contrast between where she was and where she would go in her mind when she thought of being with him.

She dreamt of him more and more as the days passed. She would be walking with the father, they would hold hands and she always felt safe. Looking up at him, her eyes would sparkle with admiration and love. They were meant to be together, she just knew it. Over time as he looked at her he would beam with pride and she could that tell he truly adored her.

On one particular day Navi felt like everything in her world of darkness was shifting. There was once again that external chaos all around her and the shouting, slamming, crying and moaning sounds all seemed amplified. Her instinct was to curl up in a ball and start sucking her thumb, fantasizing about the strong man who was always looking at her so lovingly. But this time, there was no peace in that position. Navi could feel a stretching, a pulling, a pushing.

In the chaos she heard the voice of the man calling to her, calling her by name. It sounded sweet like honey, but hard and defined, like it was being cut into stone. Navi wanted to respond to him, she wanted to find him in the light, but she was so afraid.

She was afraid to leave the darkness because it was all she had ever known. She was afraid to go out to where the shouting and wailing existed because it was so ominous. She was afraid to go to the kind father because she felt so rejected, and she thought he would eventually reject her too. But at the same time, she was afraid to stay in the darkness because she felt something pushing her out of the darkness and an even stronger force pulling her into the light.

Navi started to kick blindly at the force that seemed to be pushing against her. She would connect with it and press back with all of her might. Straining and struggling, she pushed with all of the strength in her legs and arched her back, letting her shoulders dig in against the ominous pressure.

She heard the voice of her dad shouting at her mom, "Shut up! Stop your crying! Look at the mess you've made, there's blood everywhere!"

She heard her mom's cries, "Help me, please! We have to get to the doctor! Help me! I can't hold it in, it's coming now!"

And in the midst of the commotion, she heard the still, small voice of the kind father, "It's time, my child. You are becoming Navi! Come forth, come out here into the light and see all that I have prepared for you!"

With that voice speaking, Navi felt a peace rushing all

over her and she stretched herself out. She turned over and smiled, stretching again and uncoiling. She strained so she could make herself long and tense. Bracing herself, she pushed her feet firmly against the soft walls of darkness that she was surrounded by.

"Come on, Navi, you can do it!" she heard the father saying. "You're doing so great! Let my love for you pull you out of that darkness! Come out here, into the light!"

Navi let him pull her forward and she finally broke through the darkness into a warm, viscid place where she was enveloped by flecks of sparkling light. She was mesmerized by the glowing balls swirling past her and she could feel a sloppy, thick membrane surrounding her. It was like she was suspended in space, engulfed by the sticky substance and submerged where galaxies whirled all around her.

Navi heard her mom screech a blood chilling scream and she felt a push stronger than anything she had ever felt before. She was alarmed, but not afraid, and she opened her mouth wide to let out a loud sound that was shrill like breaking glass. Just as quickly as she had entered the warm place with the flecks of light spinning around her, she was all at once pushed out into a place of only light and no darkness.

Navi's piercing cries were cutting through the atmosphere that hung heavily all around her. She clenched her eyes tightly to block out the brightness that had suddenly covered her. Her naked body felt the cold air against her skin as the sticky gunk dripped off.

Everything seemed so sharp and sterile. She heard new sounds now, beeps and clicks and many different voices. She felt a sharp pain in the center of her body and she opened her mouth to let out another loud cry. As she wailed she felt something dry and rough start to rub all over her, from the top of her head to the soles of her feet. Then, another rough material started to be wrapped around her, pulling tight like a cocoon. She didn't even try to resist it, and actually welcomed the warmth and closeness it brought. It reminded her of the darkness that she was now regretting ever leaving.

Navi was comforted in the dry cocoon and tightly closed her eyes to block out the offensively bright light. She felt herself spinning round again, but it wasn't like it had been before. She seemed much more aware of time and space now than she had been in the darkness. She could tell that she was being carried.

Navi was spun around once more and finally came to rest in the warmest place she ever could imagine. She could feel her heart pounding, but knew it was not racing like it had before. As she took notice of how her heart was beating within her, she strangely felt like she had another heart beating together with her, but somehow it was outside of her. She felt the heart within her chest and the heart outside of her catch the same rhythm and begin to beat at the same time. Dum-da-dum, dum-da-dum, dum-da-dum the hearts kept pace with one another.

There in the warmth of the heartbeat haven, she finally felt at peace. She could feel something so much bigger than herself, and it covered over her. It wasn't just warm, but also strong. It felt lovely in a way, but harsh at the same time. Navi finally had the curiosity and confidence enough to open up her eyes to see what the light around her would reveal.

She lifted her head and let the light fill her eyes. Once they adjusted to the brightness of her surroundings, she was finally able to focus on the source of that warmth and heart-beat that hovered over her. What she saw was comforting and confusing at the same time. She saw a mountain of a woman, and Navi felt small, as if she were tucked into this woman's bosom.

The woman turned her face and looked down on Navi with tears flowing from her bruised and bloodshot eyes. Her face looked sad, but her eyes had the tiniest flickers of pride and joy.

"Hello, Navi," she whispered from her chapped lips. "It's so nice to finally meet you." The tears just flowed from her eyes.

Navi was squinting and blinking, not completely sure what to think about all of this. She felt strange, like she belonged to this woman, but at the same time she felt like the woman didn't really want her. Blinking and squinting, she stared up into that huge face. She could feel the hearts beating as one and she came to realize the external heartbeat belonged to this lady.

"Navi," the woman whispered, "I'm your mama."

Navi understood. This was the mom that she had heard crying. This was the mom who she had heard being smacked. That must be why she had the bruises on her eyes.

This was the mom who had just pushed her out of the warm, wet womb and into this big, bright, scary world.

[2]
DARKNESS INTO LIGHT

NAVI WASN'T SURE OF WHAT TO THINK ABOUT THIS bright new place or this mom she had been handed over to. There was constant chaos all around and she was always being moved. She started out being wrapped up in that cocoon and given to the mountain of a mom, but before long she was shuffled off into a quiet place, and just as soon as she grew accustomed to those surroundings she woke up somewhere else.

The days ticked by quickly and they were each filled with their own drama. There were so many sounds - yelling, crying, things being broken, doors slamming shut. Navi quickly learned to be alone, but she also found that using her strong lungs to wail out a loud cry would signal the mom to bring her food or change her diaper. Navi knew that the mom loved her and that she would always feed her and change her, but she also knew that this mom had a lot of busy things going on in her life.

This mom was always tired, and she always seemed sad. There wasn't much life in her eyes, and there was always a sorrowful hopelessness about her. The bruises that had been on her eyes eventually faded but then bruises would appear on her cheeks, her shoulders, her arms.

Sometimes this mom would pick up Navi and take her to different rooms in the house or to other places completely. There was a huge, bright world filled with lots of things to see and hear and so much danger. Everything seemed harsh and scary, and there wasn't a lot of peace in Navi's little life. There was good reason to be afraid, too. The loud sounds that happened at home were usually from her dad. He always sounded so angry, like he was having a fit of rage everyday.

One night, as Navi laid on her back in her crib, she stared at the ceiling and watched the lights dancing across the room as the headlamps of passing cars shined through the window. Whoosh, whoosh, whoosh the lights would go as they crossed over her crib. She liked watching the patterns and felt soothed and comforted every time the light would zoom over her.

As she watched the light dance, a new light suddenly entered her room. This light spilled in from the doorway, which had been slowly opened and then closed. Navi felt an uneasiness creep over her as she realized a shadow was looming above her and blocking her from seeing the car's lights zoom across the ceiling.

The shadow smelled bad, like sour medicine and burnt chemicals. She could see the silhouette of a head full of messy hair and a big bushy beard. The shadow was big, it was tall and wide and much larger than the mom was.

"Hello Navi," the shadow spoke to her. "I'm your dad," it said.

Navi laid as still as she could and held her breath. The only thing she knew about this dad up until now was that he was loud, and mean, and violent. He was constantly shouting and cursing and breaking things and hitting on that mom. Navi was very afraid that he was going to do one or all of those things to her now, and she was frightened. Although she was unable to see the details of his face, she just knew he was angry. He was always angry.

The silhouette came closer to her and leaned farther over the top of the crib. "Navi, don't you want to say hello to your dad?" he asked her. Little Navi couldn't answer him even if she wanted to, but she tried hard to just stay very still.

The shadow hovered over her and came closer to her face. The pungent smell intensified as the dad leaned over the edge of the crib put his face down near Navi's. "Hey there little baby. Why won't you talk to your dad? What's wrong with you, ya little brat?" he growled. "If you won't say hi to me I won't come back to see you ever again," he threatened.

Navi didn't think that sounded too bad at all. She didn't want him to come back into her room. This dad was scary and he smelled bad. She would be just fine if he chose to stay away, but apparently he wasn't going to give up quite that easily.

Navi's dad leaned in a little closer and she saw a different shadow come across the ceiling. This time the shadow was the dad's hand and before she knew what was happening the hand was already on her face, roughly grabbing her little cheeks.

"Listen here, brat! You are my first child, you're my daughter and you're gonna grow up one day. You better not forget your old dad, because if it wasn't for me, you wouldn't even be here!" he seethed. "Navi, you're gonna grow up to be just like me, you understand? You're gonna get all these powers to read people's minds and make them do what you want them to do, just like your old dad, you hear me?" His grip had tightened on her tiny face and he was shaking her head back and forth as he spit out the words.

Navi couldn't take it anymore, she had to let out a cry. Her lungs opened up and she pushed out the loudest sound she could. The sound of her cry cut through the darkness and caused the dad to tense up.

"Stop it!" he hissed. His hand went from gripping her

cheeks to quickly covering her mouth and nose. Navi began to panic as she realized she was unable to breathe. She tried even harder to let out a scream, but to no avail. His grip on her had locked out any sound from escaping.

"Stop it, ya little brat! You're gonna have to learn that you can't act this way to your old dad!" The words were harsh and he spat at her, the whole time keeping his grip on her mouth. "I'll give you a reason to cry like a baby!" he howled.

With one swift motion he pulled his hand back and leaned all the way over the crib to put his own mouth where his hand had just been. It happened so quickly Navi wasn't able to gasp a breath before he suctioned himself to her face.

With his mouth clamped over hers, he started to let out a long, slow breath into her tiny mouth. The taste of his breath was ripe and pungent and its consistency was thick and syrupy. Quickly Navi realized this wasn't just air he was breathing into her, but a thick, dank substance that was much heavier than plain old air. Navi felt it filling her mouth, expanding as it entered her throat and windpipe and opened up her lungs, her stomach and her other organs.

The dad continued releasing the long, slow breath until Navi's entire body was filled with the thick, gooey matter. The oozy stuff permeated little Navi's whole body, from her head to her toes. It was all inside of her, filling her up everywhere. The substance seemed to ebb and flow, slithering almost as if it were alive.

When he had finally expended his breath into little Navi, the dad stood up and slowly rubbed the back of his hand across his mouth. Droplets of the goo hung from his beard and mustache, and he smeared them in as he wiped his face. There was a dreadful look set deep in his bloodshot eyes and he had an evil countenance about him. He started panting like a dog, his broad shoulders rising and falling with a marked heaviness.

Navi laid in her crib, gagging on the oozy substance, choking for air. Finally she was able to swallow hard enough to clear her airway, and as soon as she gulped in a fresh breath she once again let out a cry. The dad quickly grabbed her face again and she instantly stifled her cries and instead she laid there whimpering softly.

"I told you you're gonna grow up to be just like your old dad," he mumbled. "Now you're on the same level I'm on, and you'll be able to call on these dark powers to help you control people and get them to do whatever you want them to!" he declared to her.

Navi couldn't understand any of this. She felt so scared, so confused. She just laid in her crib, staring up at the grim face of her dad hovering over her. Her whimpers slowed to sighs, and she laid there mesmerized by the look on his face. The longer she held his gaze, the further inside of him she could see.

She looked past the glowing embers lighting up his eyes and saw deep into him, into his soul. She could see the dad as a person, not as the monster he was presenting himself to be. Deep down, this dad was a frightened little boy who had been deeply rejected and abused by his own parents, and he was living out that pain by hurting and intimidating people.

Navi pressed in and saw the moment that icky black stuff had first went into her dad. He was just a little boy, maybe four or five years old. She saw a grown man come to his bedroom late in the night and put that black evil sludge inside of him while he was laying in his bed. Her dad was sad about what had happened, but instead of telling anyone about it he kept it locked up inside, guarding it with his anger. That secret was still locked up in his heart, and his anger roared louder the closer people got to letting it out.

Navi kept staring up at her dad's face and could see even before the moment that the evil secret came to life. She could see her dad so tiny, like he wasn't even a person yet. He was just a dream, only a promise at this time.

She looked deeper until she could see where the promise was resting. It was in the hands of the Father who had helped her get pushed out of the darkness a few months earlier. She could see the face of the Father looking with such love at the tiny promise that was her dad and marveling at the great destiny that he had created for her dad to fulfill. Navi was even hidden in that destiny - she could see herself in the promise!

The longer she looked the more she could see. The story unfolded in such a grand way that she saw both before her dad was placed in the promise as well as all of the promises that would come out of her life and beyond, too.

Her dad looked down on her laying in the crib and he felt, for the first time in his sad life, feelings of repentance and remorse. He realized as he stared at his child that he had never allowed anyone to hold his gaze or look at him with anything but contempt, anger or fear.

Big tears spilled from his eyes and fell upon Navi. He wanted so badly to take back the black substance he had placed inside of his tiny daughter.

The warm tears started to wash away the black tar that was on her, but what had been put inside of her remained. The dad was troubled by that realization and hastily wiped his eyes and cleared his throat. He turned from the crib and left the room, leaving the door open. The light spilled in from the hallway and lit her room with a golden glow.

In that golden glow that rested in her room, Navi wasn't scared or afraid anymore. She had seen the promise in the hands of the Father and she knew that everything was going to be alright.

[3]

A NARROW ESCAPE

NAVI'S LIFE REVOLVED AROUND THAT CRIB FOR THE next few months. The mom would come to her room, take her out of the crib on an adventure, then put her back in. The dad would come in the room every so often late in the night, leaning over to stare at his daughter. Sometimes he would babble incoherently, sometimes he would sit in the corner of the room and fall asleep until the morning light woke him the next day.

There was always fighting, yelling, slamming and cursing in the house, and everyone just got used to that being the norm. Navi was growing quickly and learned to roll over, then crawl, stand up and walk, all the while babbling out new words nearly every day. The time passed quickly, and she was three years old in what seemed like the blink of an eye.

Right after her third birthday, Navi was sitting on her mom's lap at her grandmom's house. The mom had sad, bruised eyes again, but she also had a big, fat belly. Navi was looking at her mom and asking lots of three-year-old questions, like whys and hows. The mom was trying to explain to her that she had a new baby in her tummy and when the baby came out Navi would be a big sister.

The next day Navi's mom left and she was gone for what seemed like a really long time to Navi. The dad came to grandmom's to visit and brought their puppy Rags with him. Navi was so excited to see the puppy and she happily climbed up on the dad's lap to hold the little ball of fur. Her grandmom had just trimmed her bangs straight across her tiny forehead, and she thought Navi looked so cute that she decided to snap a photo.

The very next day, the dad took off on a long trip with the Navy. Then, a day or two later, the mom returned to the grandmom's house, carrying a little baby wrapped up tight in a receiving blanket. Navi had never seen anything so tiny and so beautiful before.

"Dat's a bay-bee," she cooed as she sweetly touched the fuzzy brown hair crowing the new princess's little head. Navi loved that new baby more than she had ever loved anything in her life.

Life started being very different for Navi, the mom and the new little baby. They stayed at the grandmom's house for a very long time, and their life seemed less chaotic and more peaceful every day. As the days and weeks passed, the baby started cooing and rolling over, then crawling, standing and walking just like Navi had done not so long ago. This baby was smart and sweet and she walked and talked much earlier than other children her age.

One day the grandmom baked a cake for the baby. Navi, the mom and some others who had started being involved with their everyday lives all came together and sang to the baby, clapping their hands and cheering as she smeared the chocolate cake all over her tiny face. Navi couldn't help but notice the mom had a sad, lonely look in her eyes as the rest of the crowd celebrated. Navi recognized that look, and she knew that whenever the mom had those sad eyes she would end up talking on the telephone for hours later in the evening.

That was exactly what happened, Navi's mom went off and spent the rest of the night with the phone pressed to her ear, speaking softly and crying to whoever was on the other end. Navi knew the mom was sad, but she couldn't understand why. They finally had a life without the yelling and slamming and bruises on her eyes. They had a nice life with the beautiful new baby and the grandmom and so many others who all seemed to love them so much. But for the mom, that didn't seem to be enough.

Time marched on and Navi had turned five years old. She was such a bright child and excelled at reading and writing. Her little sister was right behind her everywhere she went, and she copied everything Navi said or did. Life seemed to be as good as it could get, until one day when the phone rang and the mom leapt up to run and answer it.

It seemed normal at first, like the other calls she would run to. Her eyes always started out big and bright, almost as if she wanted whoever was on the other end to see how pretty she was and how happy it made her for them to call.

But this call was different. The moms eyes went from big and bright to confused and scared. She asked a few quick questions like, "When?" and "Where?" and then her eyes changed again. They turned dark and sad and she started crying a long, low wail. Her back slid down the wall as the phone fell from her hand and the volume of her cry amplified.

"Noooooooooooooo," she moaned as she collapsed in a pile on the floor.

The grandmom came rushing in, asking the mom what had happened. Through her tears and cries the mom told her what the person on the other end of the phone had said.

"He's dead," she bellowed. She said more words than that, but all Navi understood was the dead part. Dead was like when her puppy Rags had gotten sick and she had found him laying behind the garage with little white bugs crawling all over his face and side. Her granddad had gotten out a shovel and dug a hole to bury him and Navi and her little sister weren't able to play with him ever again after that.

"Dead."

That word hung heavily in the air as the grandmom placed the phone back in its cradle.

"What happened, honey?" she asked the mom.

"He hanged himself," the mom wailed. "He finally did it, just like he had threatened to all these years! It's all my fault for keeping the girls away from him."

"Now honey," the grandmom said lovingly, "he did this on his own. It had nothing to do with you and these girls. He was a sick man and this was bound to happen eventually. You were lucky that you all got away before he did it to you and the girls first!" Her face looked sad, but she seemed more concerned for the mom.

"Come over here, Navi," she said as she boosted the girl up on her lap.

"You need to think of your girls," she told the mom. "All of a sudden they only have one parent, and they will need you to be strong for them now more than ever," she said firmly.

"Look at this child! You've got her all upset and confused. Straighten yourself up and take care of her. She lost her dad today, and she needs her mom to be here for her. You've got another one asleep in the next room and she's gonna need you too."

"Come here, Navi," the mom whimpered as she took the child from the grandmom's lap.

"Your grandmom is right. We narrowly escaped with

our lives. If not for her letting us come here to stay we could have ended up dead, just like your dad," she said between sobs, tears rolling down her face.

"Now we will need to figure out how to live this life completely on our own. I'm gonna need your help taking care of your little sister," she whimpered.

"It's ok, mom," Navi said as she placed her tiny hands on her mom's little cheeks. "I love you, mom, and it's ok," she promised.

The mom didn't seem encouraged by Navi at all. She actually seemed even more upset than she was before. She put the child down and bolted out the door, the grandmom running after her.

"Where are you going?" she called.

"I just need to get away from here!" the mom answered as she jumped in her car and slammed the door. She tore out of the driveway, spraying gravel as she sped up the little hill.

Deep inside, Navi knew the mom wouldn't be back anytime soon. The grandmom scooped her up and carried her inside, speaking softly to her the whole time.

"Your mom is just dealing with a broken heart, baby. I told her from the beginning that man was capable of this and much worse. I'm just thankful he never hurt you or your little sister," she rambled as they went to the back room of the house.

She sat Navi on the couch and went to get her little

sister from the bedroom where she had been napping. All the commotion had woken her up, but she was in a happy, playful mood.

Navi slid off of the couch to sit on the floor with her and the grandmom brought them dolls to play with. In no time the little girls were off in their fantasy playtime world, dressing up their dollies and playing their innocent little games. The chaos of the day seemed to melt away as they connected with each other, and Navi quickly forgot all about the dreadful phone call and the mom driving off.

Navi may have forgotten, but the grandmom hadn't. She made her way back into the kitchen and picked up the phone to try and track her daughter down. She knew that she had been very upset when she left and she was worried about what she may do under these circumstances.

She wanted her to come back and be the mom these two little girls needed her to be. This mom was all the girls had now, and she wasn't about to let her run away from them when they needed her the most.

[4]

A SIMPLE INTRODUCTION

Navi and her little sister didn't even ask for the mom while she was away. They just let the grandmom be like their mom, and she did everything she could to keep them happy and healthy. They were well taken care of and shown lots of love while that mom was away.

But the mom did eventually return to the grandmom's. She had stayed away for a few days, but she came back before a week had passed. Navi noticed that she had bruises on her eyes again, but this time they were just underneath, not all around. And she looked very skinny, like her bones could pop right through her skin.

The grandmom quickly set herself to cooking wholesome comfort foods for the mom and setting her a place at the table so she could sit and eat. She gave her hot coffee, hot food and a nice, warm smile.

"I'm so glad you're back, honey! We all are," she beamed as she sat a big plate of meat, potatoes and gravy in front of the mom.

"Eat this up and I'll cut you a piece of the pie I baked for dessert. Do you girls want some too?" she turned and asked Navi and her sister.

The little girls climbed up to the table and sat in their chairs, waiting for the delicious food and eyeballing the mom as she quickly shoveled in one bite after the other. She kept her head down and didn't dare look at either of the girls.

Navi leaned closer to the mom and she smelled that familiar sour scent of chemicals that used to linger in the dad's beard as he hovered over her crib when they lived in the little house. The mom cocked her shoulder up and quickly scarfed down her food. She hopped up from the table, mumbling something about taking a shower as the grandmom was carrying in the two steaming bowls of food for the little girls.

"Honey, don't you want your dessert?" she asked, confused about why her daughter had left the table so quickly.

"I'll have it later, mom. Just leave me alone," she growled as she slammed the bathroom door shut.

Navi and her sister ate their food as they sat in silence. Since they were so good at eating it all up, the grandmom cut them each a piece of her homemade pie and sat down with them to enjoy a slice herself while the girls ate. She was nervous about their mom, but they would never know. Around them she was always kind and calm.

When the mom came out of the bathroom she went straight to bed, shutting and locking the door when she went into her bedroom. The grandmom made sure the little girls washed up, brushed their teeth and put on their pajamas before they climbed up in the bed they had shared since the mom had brought them there several months earlier. She tucked them in with kisses on their foreheads and made sure a nightlight was left lit before she shut the door to their tiny bedroom.

That night Navi dreamt vivid dreams. In one dream, she and her little sister were in a safe, warm home with a good mom and a good dad. Everything seemed to be going well and everyone was so happy, but one day Navi stood before her family and she opened her mouth wide. Her eyes rolled back in her head and the gooey black sludge the dad had breathed into her that night while she laid in her crib started coming out of her mouth in the dream. It was scary for everyone watching, and they all turned their heads and walked away. Navi just stood there, eyes white, head back and mouth wide, the ooze pouring out of her. The good father she had known as long as she could remember came into the room and he put his hand on her head. In an instant, her eyes came back to normal and her mouth shut. The father started cleaning her up, and the next thing she knew they were in a place where even the memory of that black gooey tar couldn't exist.

When Navi woke up the next day the mom was already gone. She stayed gone for a few days again and Navi and her sister just learned to love the grandmom like a mom instead. Everything they needed was right there, and they even had plenty of toys and dolls to play with. Life seemed to be a little more normal each day.

When the mom did return, she looked much different than she had before. This time she didn't have the dark circles under her eyes and instead she had on pretty blue eyeshadow and dark mascara. Her body wasn't skinny, either, but she looked more healthy than she had the last time she came back. She was wearing pretty jewelry and a new outfit, too. Her voice was light and sprinkled with laughter as she ran through the house chatting all about where she had been and who she had met.

"Mom, I'm telling you, this man is different! He isn't like all the losers in this awful poverty-stricken town! His family owns the market at the bottom of the hill, and he is a real businessman. You can just tell he knows what he's doing, and he drives a really nice car and has a nice house too!" The mom couldn't contain herself and just gushed on and on about her new friend.

"Navi, I'm going to take you to meet him! You need to

put on your prettiest dress, the one with the silk sash that ties in the back, okay? Hop to it, girl, go get changed!" she ordered.

Navi went to her room and quickly took off her comfy play clothes. She tugged the fancy dress off the hanger in the closet and grabbed the white tights and shiny black shoes she always wore with it. The little girl rushed back out to the living room, eager to obey the mom who seemed to be radiating excitement. When she got back to her she heard the mom bubbling over, giddy with elation. She helped Navi pull on the tights and buttoned up the back of her dress.

"Mom, he said he has been waiting for a woman like me to come into his life. He has money, houses and cars and he just wants someone to share it with. Someone he can trust!" She chattered on while tying the sash of Navi's dress.

As the little girl pulled on her patent leather mary janes, the mom grabbed a hairbrush and drug it through Navi's long brown hair.

"No time to waste, Navi! He is waiting on us, hurry up! We have to get going!" The mom jumped to her feet and headed to the door, stopping at the bathroom mirror to check and make sure her hair was fluffed just right and turning around to check the view of her backside in the painted-on jeans she wore.

Rushing out the door, she gently shoved her daughter into the car and reminded her to buckle her seat belt as they backed up to the driveway. The grandmom and Navi's little sister stood in the doorway, waving goodbye. Navi and the mom smiled and waved back and the mom gave a couple quick toots of the horn as she drove off.

Navi couldn't help but feel giddy with anticipation during the short car ride. She was so happy that things were finally going to be better, with her mom back again, just like it was supposed to be. This was the first time she could ever remember her mom truly being happy and she was glad to be included in on the excitement. Everything really was turning out for the best!

As Navi sat in the backseat and daydreamed about how perfect life was suddenly playing out, her mom pulled into the parking space in front of the convenience store at the bottom of the hill on the outskirts of town. Lowering her sun visor, she looked at herself in the mirror. She checked her makeup and touched up her lipstick as she looked at Navi's reflection, catching the child's attention with a firm, "Now you listen here, little girl."

She turned around in her seat and narrowed her eyebrows as she looked sternly at Navi. "You better be on your very best behavior when we go in here. Remember, children are to be seen and not heard! I will really let you have it if you mess this up for me, so I don't want to hear a single peep from you, little missy. And don't you dare touch anything, you hear me?"

Navi stared back at the mom with a look of shock. She

had expected this to be a fun time of them giggling together and maybe even holding hands, but the mom had just made sure it was known that she would be having none of that. She could tell by the angry look on the mom's face that she was already in trouble, and they hadn't even gotten out of the car yet. Her eyes dropped and she fixed her gaze on the buckles of her little black shoes.

"You better not blow this for me! The man likes me *and* he has money! We need this to work out so we can get out of your grandmom's, understand? So you straighten up, little girl, and act right!"

The mom unbuckled her seatbelt and lifted Navi from the seat, smoothing her hair down on her head as she stood her up in the little parking lot. She also fluffed out her own hair a little more and smoothed her hands down the backside of her skin tight jeans before sashaying through the door, Navi following at her heels.

"Hey there big fella," she purred at the man behind the counter.

"There's my sexy girl!" the man exclaimed, coming around from the cash register so he could wrap his arms around her and give her a big, passionate kiss. The man slid his hand up the back of that mom's head, twisting up his fingers in her hair. Navi looked away as they locked lips, feeling embarrassed to see them sticking their tongues in each others' mouths.

They pulled themselves apart and the mom told this new man, "This is Navi, my oldest daughter."

"She's so pretty!" the man gushed. "And she's a big girl, too. How old are you, Navi?" he asked.

Navi knew better than to pipe up. She just kept her gaze down, staring at those shiny shoes. She didn't want to ruin this for the mom. This was important.

"Navi, you answer him when he talks to you!" the mom said shrilly.

The little girl was so confused. Was she supposed to keep her mouth shut? Or was she supposed to answer the question? She could feel her heart pounding in her throat and her nerves racing up and down her body.

"Five," she whispered at a low tone that was nearly inaudible.

"What's that? What did you say, honey?" the man inquired.

Navi didn't know to answer him or only answer the mom at this point.

"Speak up, child!" the mom growled at her, smacking her on the back.

"I'm five years old," Navi said aloud, her eyes still fixed toward the floor.

"Oh, you are a big girl!" the man replied. "Do you like candy, Navi?"

The child slowly nodded her head up and down.

"Come over here, we have all the best candy bars in our

cooler. Take whichever is your most favorite," he coaxed her.

Navi peered down into the chest freezer and saw the candy bars in little white wire baskets. She slid the glass lid to the side and pulled out a cold little package. The man and the mom were focused on each other, which was a huge relief. Navi would have done anything to get the attention off of her at that time.

She carefully pulled the paper off of the chocolate covered candy and bit into the crunchy, caramel-ly goodness. The candy was frozen solid and hard as a rock. This turned out to be a huge disaster, because as Navi attempted to bite through it, she ended up breaking off a piece of her tooth. She dropped the frozen candy on the floor and let out a cry, covering her sore mouth with both hands.

"What did you do?" shouted the mom from across the little store. She came to Navi's side and cupped her chin in her hand, lifting her little face up to get a better look at her.

"Oh my goodness! She's broken her tooth!" she exclaimed. "Let me get her up to my mom's, she'll know what to do about this," she said, panicking.

Suddenly Navi's life turned into chaos once again, as the mom picked her up and spun her around, bumping into the man awkwardly as they both rushed to get out of the store. There was a flurry of emotion and some quick words exchanged by the adults, and before she knew it, Navi was being tossed into the backseat of the mom's car.

She kept her hand over her sore mouth, trying to protect the broken tooth from further damage. The mom jumped into the driver's seat and sped off before Navi had buckled her seatbelt.

"You spoiled little brat!" she seethed at Navi. " I should have known better than to drag you along! You ruin everything! If this doesn't work out now it will be all your fault!" she growled, scathing.

"You just couldn't stand not being the center of attention, could you? Well you got your wish, you little heathen! Now I'll have to go back and try to clean up the mess you've made of the most important relationship of my life!" the mom berated her the whole trip back to the grandmom's.

"It was just supposed to be a simple introduction. He was supposed to see that having you in the picture wouldn't make things more complicated. Now he probably wants nothing to do with me! Who would volunteer to spend their days with a whiny brat?"

Navi just kept whimpering with her hands clasped tightly over her face. When they got to the grandmom's she ran inside to show her what had happened. Grandmom knew just what to do and grabbed a washcloth and an icepack for Navi to hold on her mouth. The mom stormed through the room, slamming the door to her bedroom.

Navi's tears dried up as she sat in the kitchen chair, looking at her pretty dress. She knew she had been a very bad girl and she regretted even going to the store with the mom in the first place.

She hoped she would get another chance to make the mom proud. She hoped she would get to meet the mom's new friend again. She knew if she got another chance she wouldn't mess things up next time.

Some rest, lay and sleep.
Others stretch, awaken and stir;
Ready to KILL for food.

[5]
MOVIN' ON UP

NAVI SOON GOT HER CHANCE TO IMPRESS THE MOM'S new friend. In less than a week the mom came home in a whirlwind again, gushing about that man and going on and on about how he was making her his girlfriend. She brought empty boxes and bags with her and told Navi and her little sister to fill them up with all of their belongings.

Navi didn't really understand what moving meant, and she didn't really have very many belongings, but she and her little sister took the boxes and bags to their tiny bedroom and started putting their clothes, toys and games in them. They could hear the mom telling the grandmom about how lucky she was that this man was moving her and the girls out-of-state to a nice home in a big city.

"Out-of-state? Why in the world do you have to move so

far away? Can't he just run that store for his parents so you can stay in town?" the grandmom protested.

The mom quickly countered everything the grandmom brought up.

"Mom, no one in this poverty-ridden town is ever going to have a good life! He wants to give me a better life, and he said he is happy to take care of the girls, too! He is a businessman, mom. A successful one! And he has a job waiting for him in the city we are moving to."

Navi and her little sister came from their bedroom, dragging their overstuffed boxes and bags behind them. Picking up on the mom's excitement, they felt giddy, too. Navi really didn't know what it meant to be a businessman, but she hoped this man was able to forget all about the fiasco that happened when they had first met.

"Honey, what are you going to do? Just load up your car and drive off? This is all happening awfully fast. Moving out-of-state?" the grandmom strained to make her point.

"Mom, you will never understand!" the mom quipped. "I am taking the girls and what little we have and we are moving away. This is what is best for me! I will finally have a chance at a better life. You can either argue with me about it or you can share in the excitement and tell us all goodbye."

"You know I want what's best for you. I just want time for this to all sink in. It's moving so fast, and you just barely met this man," the grandmom protested, choking back her tears.

"Well, mom, you're not getting more time. He's at the bottom of the hill waiting in the moving truck. Tell the girls goodbye, you'll miss them when they're gone," that mom chided hastily.

"Come here girls, let me give you goodbye kisses," the grandmom said, tears rolling down her cheeks.

Navi took the grandmom's sad, troubled face between her tiny hands. "Don't be sad, grandmom, we will be good girls. And we love you so, so much!" she told her, looking into her big, sad eyes.

"Yeah!" added the little sister. "We love you so much!"

The grandmom took all the time she was allowed to kiss the girls goodbye and tell them how precious they were to her. She whispered in their ears about how beautiful they were, about how smart they were, about how proud she was of them. And before she knew it, the mom had stuffed the final item into her car and announced it was time to go.

Navi and her little sister were ushered out the door and strapped into the backseat of the car. The mom gave her normal toot-toot of the horn as she sped out of the driveway, arm stuck out the window, frantically waving as the grandmom and granddad stood crying on the porch, bewildered and in shock.

By the time they made it to the little shop at the edge of town, the man was out of the moving truck, pacing back and forth. "What took you so long? I thought you weren't coming back!" he shouted at the mom as she pulled into the parking lot and jumped out of her car.

She grabbed him around the middle and looked lovingly into his eyes. "You knew I would come back! I had to wrestle the girls away from my mom." she told him.

"Well, I'm glad you finally got here and brought them both with you," he told her, his rough face softening just a bit.

"We have a good eight to ten hour drive ahead of us today. Why don't you let little Navi ride with me this first leg so I don't get too lonely?" he asked.

"Of course!" the mom told him, batting her big, blue eyes. She looked back over her shoulder at the car that sat idling in the entrance to the parking lot. "Navi, you're riding with Mr. Earl today, so get up in that truck. You be a good girl and don't cause any trouble for him!"

Navi unbuckled her seat belt and grabbed her dolly as she slid out of the car and walked over to where her mom and the big man stood.

"You don't need this thing," her mom said hastily as she grabbed the doll from her grip. "I told you to be on your best behavior, and we don't need you messing around with a bunch of silly toys while Mr. Earl is trying to drive this big truck!" she grumbled.

The big man squatted down so he was at eye level with Navi. "Are you ready for an adventure, little girl? I'm gonna make sure this trip is fun for you! This will be a time you'll never, ever forget!" he said to her, his eyes glistening.

Navi nodded her head and kept her mouth shut. She had learned enough the last time to remember 'children are to be seen and not heard.'

"C'mon, let's get up in my big truck," the man said, turning the little girl around so she was facing the metal ladder of stairs that led to the big, ominous door of the giant moving truck.

"Move it on up there," he said as he boosted her little bottom just enough to get up the stairs and into the passenger seat.

"That's my big girl!" he crowed at her, giving her a proud smile that made her heart skip.

"You be a good girl!" the mom called to Navi as she made her way back to the car. "I don't want to hear that you gave Mr. Earl any trouble!" she added.

As Mr. Earl climbed into the driver's seat and shut the door to the big truck, Navi felt a rush of excitement. She was looking forward to this adventure and she was going to do all she could to make up for the disaster she had caused when they had first been introduced.

"You ready to go, baby?" he asked her.

Navi nodded, happy he was including her but in the back of her mind she wasn't sure why he called her 'baby.' She wasn't the baby, she was actually the big sister. The other one was the baby.

The truck pulled out first and the mom and little sister followed close behind in their little car. As the man drove, Navi stared at him and tried to memorize everything about him. She knew the mom really, really liked him and Navi wanted to be sure she could recognize everything about this man, a man who a woman like her mom would fall in love with.

First, she noticed that he had a big, round face with lots of reddish-blonde whiskers. She also took note of his feathered hair that he would nervously run his fingers through every so often. She saw that he was a big man, with a round belly that the seatbelt was stretched taut across. Navi made sure to remember that he had freckles on his face and hands, and they were a dark shade of reddish-brown, while his skin was pale and white. There were little, wet dots sparkling along his brow and he breathed in puffs - in and out, in and out.

As the truck rumbled down the highway, Mr. Earl seemed nervous and unsure of himself. He kept clearing his throat and anxiously checking his back and side mirrors. He wanted Navi to like him, and he didn't have much experience with little girls.

The truck went over a big bump in the road and Navi's little body bounced off of her seat.

"Did you feel that?" Mr. Earl asked her.

"Yes," Navi laughed.

"Did you like it? Did it feel good?" he probed as he took his eyes from the road and looked at her.

"Yes, I like bouncing!" she answered. She was eager to make him like her, and he was giving her the attention she so desperately craved.

"I like it when you bounce up and down," Mr. Earl told her. "When we get to our new house I'll show you a fun game where you can bounce a lot!"

"That sounds fun," Navi answered, suddenly not sure about how she felt towards Mr. Earl. She became very quiet and stared out the window, watching the trees and buildings zoom by.

Their journey out-of-state had only just begun, but Navi felt further from the grandmom than ever before.

[6]
ALONG THE WAY

Out-of-state was a far, far drive. It was a very long day and Navi was hot, tired and hungry after many hours of bouncing around on the big seat of the moving truck.

They weren't able to make the entire journey in just one day and the mom and Mr. Earl decided to find a motel to stay at along the way. They stopped at an old building next to the interstate that had long rows of rooms and a big, brightly lit truck stop and restaurant out front. Navi and her little sister were happy that there were chicken nuggets and french fries on the menu and they both quickly scarfed down their food. All throughout the meal the two adults muttered back and forth about what an unexpected expense this was and how costly the dinner and the room were.

After supper the group made their way down the long sidewalk along the building and found their hotel room. It was tiny, with two lumpy beds covered in greasy, printed comforters. A big neon sign pointed its arrow right in their window and flashed on and off incessantly.

Once they got settled in, Mr. Earl locked himself in the bathroom and the mom pulled Navi aside for a little talk. "Listen, little girl. We thought we would be able to make it all the way in one day, but gas, food and lodging were way more than we had budgeted for. I need to go out for just a little bit tonite, and I need you to make sure your little sister goes to sleep and doesn't bug Mr. Earl once I leave the room, okay?"

Navi looked back at the mom with big, round eyes and slowly nodded her head up and down. She didn't know what she meant when she talked about budgeting for gas and food, but she did know how to make sure her little sister went to sleep without throwing a fit or causing any trouble for Mr. Earl. She didn't understand why the mom had to go out either, but she was going to try very hard to be a good girl.

The mom quickly changed her clothes into a little skirt and a shimmery tank top and stood in front of the mirror to tease up her hair with a comb. She dusted her cheeks and forehead with pale powder, but she made her eyes and lips darker with her lipstick and mascara. As she leaned over to buckle the tiny ankle straps on her high heels, Mr. Earl emerged from the bathroom.

It was quickly obvious that he was in there so long because he had been in the shower. The sharp scent of soap and toothpaste hung in the thick, steamy air that poured into the room. His hair was still wet and slicked back on his head, and he was wrapped in his big, blue terrycloth robe.

"Wow, look at you!" he exclaimed as his eyes fell on the mom. "You're definitely going to do well out there tonite," he told her, grabbing her around the waist and pulling her close.

"I am not looking forward to this," the mom responded. "I just want to get it over with as quickly as possible. I still can't believe you forgot to go to the bank to get extra cash for this trip."

"I had so much to do before we left! All the phone calls to make sure everything is ready for us when we get to town tomorrow, taking care of stuff at the store, plus packing everything up. Keep in mind, we probably only need about $250. You should be able to get that pretty quickly," Mr. Earl told her reassuringly as he rubbed his hand along her lower back.

"Okay, then. I'm going out, girls. Be good and get to sleep," she said flatly, patting their heads before slipping out of the door into the night.

As the door shut, the atmosphere of the room seemed to

change. The air that had been thick and heavy with shower steam seemed to quickly turn cold and sterile. Mr. Earl tugged at the curtains on the window and snapped off the light switch so that the only light shining in the room was from the lamp on the nightstand next to the bed that he sat down on.

The little girls went into the bathroom, brushed their teeth and changed into their nightgowns. When they came out of the bathroom, Navi nudged her little sister toward one of the lumpy beds and handed her a babydoll.

As the child climbed into the bed, Navi tucked the covers around her and kissed her on the forehead just like the grandmom used to do every night. She told her to go to sleep, and to have sweet dreams. Even though Navi was only three years older than her little sister, she had such a great responsibility to her and she felt like a big girl to be in charge and tuck her in at night.

Her little sister closed her eyes tightly and snuggled the babydoll to her chest. She was all wrapped up in the bedding with her little head resting on the pillow. Navi sat on the edge of the bed and stared at her, watching her breathe in and out. She waited a long time to be sure she was really asleep before she stood up.

Mr. Earl had been staring at Navi the whole time. It made her feel funny, like when she was bouncing up and down in the big moving truck and he had told her about the game he wanted to play with her.

"Come here, Navi," he said to her softly, his voice

cracking just a bit. He patted his hand on a spot next to him on the bed.

Navi could feel her heart pounding in her throat. She didn't know why she was so scared, but suddenly a terror started washing over her. She wanted to run into the bathroom and lock the door behind her, but she knew if she disobeyed Mr. Earl he would tell the mom and then for sure she would get in trouble. She timidly made her way over to where he was patting his hand.

As Navi sat down on the lumpy bed, she felt the unmistakable, overwhelming sensation of safety, love and hope that always radiated from the Father who she had known since before she was born. When she put her bottom on the bed, instead of looking to the left where Mr. Earl was sitting, Navi looked to the right and saw the indentation of the Father sitting on the mattress next to her.

She heard a voice speaking, and chose to believe it was *that* Father speaking to her, not Mr. Earl. Navi turned all of her attention to Him, and she pressed in until she could see Him sitting next to her on that lumpy hotel bed.

"I know you've been waiting for a dad, haven't you, Navi?" the Father asked her in pure innocence, with absolutely no ulterior motives.

"Yes! I would love to have a dad, just like the other little girls I know," replied Navi, excited at the opportunities this discussion presented.

"Good, because I want to be your dad," He told her.

"Thank you, this is my dream come true!" Navi exclaimed, delighted to be able to spend this precious time with her Father.

"Navi, you're my daughter, and I have a special love for you. This love is a secret, sacred love, between Father and daughter, and I don't want you to hide it. I want everyone who sees you to know that you have received my love. I am going to mark you with my love so it is obvious to everyone that you belong to me," He said to her with great care and compassion.

"That makes me so happy, Father!" Navi beamed.

"I want you to always come to this place with me, daughter. I have so much love to give you, and so many things to show you about your destiny in My Kingdom," the Father reassured her.

Navi was so content to lay there with Him. She rested her head on His chest and allowed their breathing to come into sync, and then their hearts started to beat in time with each other, ba-boom, ba-boom, ba-boom; just like her heart had been beating with the mom's heart so many years ago.

Navi felt a tinge of sadness break through when she thought of her heart beating with the mom's. It had been many years since they had shared that closeness, and she longed for the connection with her again.

Knowing the inner turmoil she was experiencing, the Father so lovingly brought reassurance to Navi. As she laid on her side, curled in a ball, He placed His enormous hand over her, stretching from her knees to the top of her head.

"Be at peace, my child," He spoke over her. The gravity of His words dug a burrow for her to snuggle down inside of, and she found herself far removed from the cares of this world. Navi indeed found peace.

She didn't even stir when the mom came back and erupted in a fit of rage after finding her curled up, asleep in Mr. Earl's bed.

"Good morning girls," the mom said sweetly to little Navi and her sister. "I have good news - you're both going to ride the rest of the way with me!" she told them.

The mom had obviously woken up very early, washed all the makeup off of her face and changed into ragged jeans and a faded tee shirt before the girls woke up. She had her hair pulled back from her pale face and she smiled softly at the children as they stretched in their bed. Navi noticed that even though her voice was light and sounded happy, her brow was furrowed and her face seemed sad.

As soon as she made the announcement, the mom quickly looked over her shoulder to watch Mr. Earl emerge from the bathroom, wrapped in his worn, blue terrycloth robe with his wet hair again slicked back from his forehead. He immediately questioned the mom about both girls riding with her. He told her he would get lonely, he reminded her that it was a long trip, he reiterated how important it was for the girls to bond with him before they all made their home together.

The mom firmly replied to each of the protests Mr. Earl presented with short answers.

"No, they will ride with me."

"You have a radio to listen to."

"There will be plenty of time to bond in the new town."

"No, they will both ride with me."

The tension was heavy in the air as the mom had the children change clothes and quickly gather their things before leading the two girls out to her car. She put what little luggage they had into her trunk and as she slammed the lid closed she puffed out a long, slow breath from between her pursed lips.

They quickly settled in and Navi and her little sister both felt so lucky to get to ride in the car with the mom when they pulled out of the motel parking lot. They knew that they were on an adventure!

Once they were out on the highway the mom fished two cereal bars out from her big purse and handed them back to Navi. Without being told what to do, the young girl opened one of them and handed it to her sister, then opened the other for herself. They munched on the berry flavored breakfast bars in silence as they watched the trees whiz by out the window.

Navi was thinking of all the things that had happened the night before. She remembered so vividly the Father speaking lovingly to her, but she also had an odd, fading memory of Mr. Earl talking to her as well.

"I have a question," she suddenly said to the mom, breaking through the silence and causing her to drift out of the lane just a bit due to the disturbance.

"What is it, Navi?" the mom answered tersely.

"Is Mr. Earl our new dad?" Navi asked.

"Why are you asking that? Do you like him? Do you want him to be your new dad?" the mom replied with a slight lilt to her voice.

Navi thought about the questions the mom had rattled off. She knew it was important to the mom that she liked Mr. Earl, and she wanted to make sure to please the mom, especially since they were spending this special adventure time together, so she answered, "Um, yeah, I think I like him. I know he likes me, too, because he told me so and said I am very special to him."

The mom gripped the steering wheel tightly and Navi saw in the reflection of the rearview mirror that her forehead was crinkled and her lips tightly pressed together.

"Oh he said that, did he?" she muttered.

"Yeah, we were playing grown up games last night when you were gone. He told me I was growing up fast and he was gonna help me be a lady like you." Navi smiled at the mirror, hoping the mom would look back at her with pride, but instead she kept her glaring eyes glued to the road ahead.

"Well, Mr. Earl needs to think about how to keep a lady like me happy before he gets concerned about teaching you anything, little girl," she said curtly. "And you need to be careful how much you run your mouth, because he has everything set up for us in this new city and we will finally have all the nice things we can't get back home. Once we move into our big, beautiful new house and start driving around in new cars, dressed up in our nice clothes - when all that starts happening you will need to keep your big mouth shut. I don't want you saying anything that will mess this up, do you understand?"

Navi could tell the mom was getting angrier with each word she said, and she was worried that she had totally ruined the fun adventure they were on by asking too many questions. She decided to take the mom's advice.

Staring out the window and watching the trees whizzing by, she made the simple decision to do just that, keep her mouth shut.

Navi and her little sister napped on and off as the road wore on. They played the "I spy" car game and told silly jokes and stories to each other to pass the time. Every so often the mom would stop at a gas station or truck stop along the way and they would all get out to stretch their legs and go potty.

Whenever they stopped Mr. Earl was always there,

too, but it seemed like the mom was making sure the girls didn't talk with him. As soon as they finished up in the restroom, she would load them back into the car with explicit instructions not to talk to anyone, then she would duck back into the store, returning after a few minutes with a plastic bag filled with snacks and drinks and Mr. Earl walking alongside her with his arm around her waist or his hand in the back pocket of her jeans. The mom would always be laughing, tossing her head back and letting her hair swish back and forth as she walked toward the car.

As she leaned up against the driver's door at the early evening stop Navi and her little sister could hear the conversation between her and Mr. Earl.

"Why don't you let one of the girls ride with me now? It's been a long, lonely day and I've been listening to the same boring songs on the radio over and over."

The mom answered, "I'm not sure, I think maybe they should both be with me so they are together, ya know? This is a big transition for them and they're so young..." Her voice seemed to trail off as she looked at her shoes and dropped her defenses.

Mr. Earl was quick to reply, "I know they're young, and they're going through a lot with this big move. Since Navi is a little older and can understand better about what is going on, you should let her ride with me the rest of the way so you can talk with your youngest. It will be good for everyone involved, and you know how important it is that we all see each other as family, right?"

"Yeah, I know," the mom replied, "I guess it would be ok for her to ride the last couple hours with you. Go get in the truck and I'll drive around and drop her off."

"Great idea, Babe!" Mr. Earl exclaimed as he smacked her bottom and kissed her fast and hard on the lips. He scurried off to get the truck running and the mom turned around to get into the driver's seat and start her car.

Navi and her little sister didn't say anything to the mom, and she didn't say anything to them as she shifted the car into drive and slowly ambled around the gas pumps to where Mr. Earl was waiting with the big moving truck.

"Here Navi, take this and go get in with him for the rest of the ride," The mom reached back toward Navi without looking over her shoulder and handed her a small juice box and a little lunch cake snack wrapped in cellophane.

Suddenly Navi had a lump in her throat. She swallowed hard and felt her throat tighten even more as her heart began to race. She was so confused, and was pondering how just this morning the mom had been so harsh with her concerning Mr. Earl, and now she was making her be alone with him again.

"Move it, girl. Get outta this car right now," the mom growled from between her clenched teeth.

With no further hesitation Navi unbuckled her seat belt and pulled the big handle to open the door and slide out of the car. Mr. Earl had the big truck running and the passenger door flung wide, so all Navi had to do was make her way up the ladder-like steps to get into the rig. Once she got onto the big seat Mr. Earl reached over her to grab ahold of the door, giving a quick wink and a wave to the mom before slamming it shut.

"Well Hello, Navi." he said sweetly, his big hand patting her tiny knee. "Thanks for coming along to ride with me."

"You're welcome," she squeaked out over the apple-sized lump in her throat, her manners getting the best of her.

Mr. Earl pulled her over to the spot in the middle of the long bench seat and fastened her seatbelt. "You'll feel safer over here next to me, it's getting dark out." he smiled at her a weird smirk and then started to drive, pulling out of the parking lot and onto the street.

Navi couldn't see over the dashboard and all she could see through the side window was the flash of streetlights or neon signs that were flickering on as the sky grew an inky dark blue. She was still swallowing past the lump and as she bounced up and down on the springy seat she felt her stomach start to flip and spin. All she could do to brace herself was lean over and rest her head against Mr. Earl, so that's what she did.

He responded to her burrowing into his side by letting out a soft moan that almost sounded like a tomcat's purr and he placed his big arm around her. In a strange way, Navi felt both unsafe and protected at the same time. It was almost as if Mr. Earl was there to defend her, but she knew he was the reason for the lump in her throat.

Not really knowing what else to do, Navi nestled in closer and drifted off to sleep with Mr. Earl's big arm wrapped around her.

[7]
FITS OF RAGE

WHEN SHE WOKE UP, NAVI WASN'T CURLED UP NEXT TO
Mr. Earl on the seat of the big truck anymore. Instead, she
was laying on a pallet of blankets on the floor of a dingy
motel in a city she had never heard of. As she blinked her
eyes to adjust to the darkness she saw flashes of light zoom
by, causing the thin drapes drawn over the room's one little
window to light up with a bright white light only to go dark
a moment later, pulsating almost as fast as a heartbeat.

Navi was unsure of her surroundings, but she knew her
little sister was laying next to her there on the floor. She
could hear the voices of the mom and Mr. Earl speaking just
above a whisper as they squeaked and creaked around on
the rackety bed just above her head.

"I thought you were going to have everything set up for
us when we got here, but instead we had to scrape up what

little money we had left to get this crappy room for the night!" the mom seethed through what Navi pictured as angry, clenched teeth.

"Just trust me, I will take care of everything once we get settled. We just had way more expenses than I expected on the front end of the move. That truck, gas, food - you know all of those things add up to a pretty penny. But I have a primo job waiting for me here and I already have some great connections with other businessmen who can hardly wait to meet you and the girls."

Mr. Earl tried to sound genuine and convincing, but there seemed to be an underlying sleaziness to what he was saying.

The mom grunted and rolled over in the lumpy bed. Navi imagined her yanking the covers around herself as she did.

This certainly was not part of the plan.

It was a fitful night without much rest. Mr. Earl and the mom tossed and turned all night long and Navi and her little sister woke and stirred at every creak and crack of the rusty bed springs. When the sun finally came up the zooming by of the cars outside was known only by sound since the rectangle of fabric covering the window was fully illuminated - a sign that it was time to get up and stop trying to sleep.

The adults were first, rolling out of the bed one at a time and wandering into the bathroom. When they finished,

Navi and her little sister went into the bathroom together. They saw a really big, gross cockroach in the bathtub and that made them hurry up and get back in the other room quickly. When they got out there the mom had the window covering pulled back and stood next to it, smoking a long brown cigarette and drinking coffee from a white styrofoam cup.

The girls had slept in the clothes they had worn the day before and the mom tossed a brown plastic grocery bag at them and told them to hurry up and get changed before Mr. Earl came back. Quickly stripping down to their panties, they slipped into the clean shorts and t-shirts and crammed their dirty clothes into the bag just as Mr. Earl came through the door.

"Alright, I got it worked out that we can stay here for a few more days and pay as we go, so you'll just need to do a little night work to get us by. I called the new office and I won't get set up to start there for another week or two." He delivered the news matter-of-factly but the mom looked at him as if he had smacked her across the face.

"You must be kidding me!" she seethed at him. "This is NOT how things are supposed to be working out! We are supposed to have a new house, a new car, a new job - remember? You said you would be bringing us here so we can have all the things we would never have been able to get back home."

"Now listen," Mr. Earl curled his arm around the

mom's waist as he curled the sides of his lips up into a little grin. "We are gonna get through this, it's just a minor set-back. Once we get up and running you'll see, things will be better. We just hit a couple bumps in the road, but in a few weeks you will be so happy you didn't give up. Remember how much fun we had when we first started dating, how eager you were to make a life with me? Well, now it's finally happening and we are doing all those things we had planned. Just help me out the next few days and I will help you and your girls out for years to come, I promise."

For some reason when Mr. Earl looked the mom in the eyes and pressed his big, fat belly up against her, it made her like jelly. Navi had never witnessed the mom swoon over a man before and she didn't really understand why she blushed and twirled her hair and batted her eyes at Mr. Earl.

"Okay, I will try to trust you. We can do this together, but please, let's try to only stay here for another week at the most."

"No!" shouted Navi, out of the blue. "We can't stay here, there's a big, yucky bug in the bathroom! And there isn't a bed for me and sissy to sleep in so at night that bug will get on us." she protested.

The mom and Mr. Earl looked at the little girl with shock apparent on their faces. It was obvious that she was scared and that she was willing to risk getting in trouble for correcting the adults, and that seemed to be the last straw for the mom. With one sudden stride she was across the room, snatching up the child.

"Listen here little girl!" she screamed at Navi. "You don't back-talk us, and you don't make the rules! This will be the last time you speak out of turn and the last time you run your little mouth, understand? Children are to be seen and not heard. One more sideways word out of you and you'll be sorry!"

At this, the mom had Navi dangling by one arm and was shaking her and screaming at full volume in her face. Navi went limp and pale, staring back at the mom in total shock. The mom's voice seemed to boom off of the walls and ceiling and bounce around the room, creating an echo within an even deeper echo. Once she stopped shaking the girl and screaming, she dropped Navi on the tattered carpet and stomped out of the room, slamming the door so hard everything seemed to shake.

"Look what you've done now you little brat!" Mr. Earl spat at her as he ran out the door in hot pursuit of the mom.

Navi didn't want to start crying because she was afraid there was no way the gush of tears would ever stop. That didn't stop her little sister from crying though, and that tiny girl sat on the carpet and started bawling like a baby. Navi just folded up and pulled her knees into her chest and laid very still with her eyes closed tight, trying to shut out the wailing of her little sister and trying to stop the awful ringing in her ears.

The chills that were running up and down her spine were suddenly warmed as a sweet presence came near.

"Hello, Navi," the Father said sweetly as He stood over her. He looked down on her with love, and with pride and joy, just like a dad would look at his little girl.

"Hi," Navi whispered.

The Father came and sat on the floor next to her. "Be encouraged my child. I want you to be fearless," He said to her as He held her hands and looked deeply into her eyes.

"You are about to go through times where your mind will try to tell you to be afraid, but I want you to be brave. It will not make sense to you now, but a day is coming soon when everything that you are about to go through will be used to bring many, many other little girls into my Kingdom!"

Navi answered Him in a tiny, mousy voice, "Okay, Father. I can be brave for you, just please don't leave me."

"Ah! Navi, I will never, ever leave you! Don't look away from me, no matter what. I will always, always be with you."

That small word of encouragement was all it took to give Navi the strength to rise up from the fetal position she had wrapped herself into. She gathered herself together and went over to her crying little sister and knelt down next to the child.

"There, there sissy," she comforted her. "Don't worry or cry anymore. Everything will be alright. The Father said He is always gonna be here with us and we should be brave and strong."

Navi's little sister didn't understand anything that she was saying to her. She had never known of a father and didn't have a reference point to compare this concept to. But she did know Navi was gaining confidence. Just seeing her sitting there on her knees, fully composed in spite of the mom's outburst just moments before gave the young child enough peace to slow her sobs and wipe her tears.

Navi and her little sister made a pact that day that no matter what ever happened, they were not going to cry about it and they would be strong and brave. Navi knew this was pleasing the Father and her little sister was going to be the first of many other little girls she would be bringing into His Kingdom.

Some hide, afraid, alone and scared
Others attack and search slyly;
Ready to spring on anything around.

[8]
STRONG AND BRAVE

IT DIDN'T TAKE MANY NIGHTS FOR THE MOM TO EARN
enough money for them to move out of the dingy hotel and
into the two bedroom apartment she had been going on and
on about everyday since they had arrived in the small South
Texas city. Navi and her little sister were so happy to be
able to sleep on the floor in their own empty little room
instead of alongside the rusty, squeaky springs underneath
of the old hotel bed. They had heard that incessant
squeaking over their heads every single night as they laid on
the floor of that dark motel room.

Navi knew what made the bed squeak. There had
been times when the mom and little sister had gone out for
an afternoon to pick up some food or go to the laundromat
and Mr. Earl would have her come over and lay on the bed
next to him. He never touched her, but he would have her

lay there in her panties, staring up at the ceiling. Mr. Earl would lay on his back under the covers and just look over at her and, before long, he would have that rusty, squeaky old bed bouncing up and down, squeak, squeak, squeaking.

Knowing that the Father told her to be brave and strong, Navi tried to think of him during those times, not what weird, old Mr. Earl was doing to himself under the covers. The girl was able to block out what was going on around her most of the time and just converse with the Father. He would tell her how pretty she was, or how proud he was of her and encourage her to keep being strong.

Now that they were in the apartment instead of the motel, Navi was hoping she wouldn't have to lay next to Mr. Earl wearing just her panties anymore. Since the mom was gone almost all night long every single night, Navi and her little sister would stay in their room and try to just be quiet and go to sleep so they wouldn't upset the grown-ups. Sometimes, as the sun was peeking around the corners of the blanket that had been tacked up around their bedroom window, they would wake up to see the mom sitting in a folding chair, quietly staring at them as she smoked a long, brown cigarette.

During these days things were probably what would be thought of as pretty normal in their little household. The mom slept nearly from sun-up to sun-down each day so she was able to work every night and Mr. Earl would watch television in the living room while the little girls would play with crayons or baby dolls.

When the mom did wake up the strained conversation between her and Mr. Earl was usually based around what they were going to have for dinner and what time she thought she would be home. Mr. Earl would always lie to her and say he had been making phone calls all day long to try and find out where their new furniture was, or why his office wasn't ready or what they needed to do to get Navi enrolled in school.

Navi knew Mr. Earl was lying because he never called anyone during the day while the mom was asleep. All he did was watch the same boring television shows for hours everyday and sometimes when her little sister would go to their bedroom to take a nap he would have Navi strip down to her panties and come sit next to him on the couch while he covered his lap with a blanket and made the couch springs squeak just like the rusty motel bed used to do.

One morning when the mom came home she was so proud and excited to show Navi and her little sister that she had bought something fancy the night before. It was a long, slender black box that she sat next to the tv set. She asked the girls if they knew what that was, and of course they both shook their heads and looked at her doe-eyed. Overflowing with excitement, the mom pulled something else from her crumpled paper bag. The girls instantly recognized the popular cartoon characters on the cover and the mom opened the case and took out the clumsy looking tape. Popping it into the slim black VCR, her countenance glowed as she watched her daughters' faces light up when the cartoon started to play.

"Now girls, there are three more movies for you in here, so when you get finished with that one you can watch another, okay?" she said with a strange sweetness they hadn't heard in many weeks.

"What did you bring for me, baby?" Mr. Earl inquired of the mom with his arm wrapped around her slim waist.

"Oh, don't you worry, I've got ours right here," the mom cooed back at him with her bedroom voice. She lifted a bag twice the size as the one the cartoons had come in and handed it to Mr. Earl.

"We should watch one of these in a little while as soon as they go to bed. It will help me get in the mood to really make some good money tonite!" she said with a sparkle in her eye.

~~~

IT QUICKLY BECAME a daily event for the girls to watch one of their movie tapes after they ate their peanut butter sandwich lunches. It never seemed to take long for Navi's little sister to fall asleep as they watched the cartoon adventures.

One day, right after she went to sleep, Mr. Earl picked her up and carried her into the girls' little bedroom and quietly shut the door. He crept back into the living room and stood in front of the television, completely blocking Navi's view of the cartoon.

"Hey, I'm trying to watch that!" Navi said defiantly. She didn't really like Mr. Earl, and she had lost any shred of respect she may have had for him after hearing him lie to the mom so many times.

"It's okay, Navi. I'm gonna let you keep watching movies, but I'm just gonna show you a different one now, alright?" he answered her in an esoteric tone. "Come with me and I'll let you pick out which one you want to watch."

Mr. Earl led Navi to the closet in he and the mom's bedroom and opened the bifold door. He lifted the little girl up and she was suddenly eye-level with the top shelf where there were about twenty puffy plastic videocassette cases lined up along the wall.

"Go ahead, Navi, pick any one you want," he said nervously. "Hurry up."

Navi didn't know what any of these movies were about but the edges she could see of the cases resembled the cartoons she and her sister watched everyday. She looked down the row and pointed to one of the boxes that had big, pink letters down the spine.

"Oh, that is a very good choice!" Mr. Earl said excitedly as he pulled the tape from the row. "Come on, let's go watch it together!" he said as he spun her around to his hip and carried her into the living room. He was suddenly being so playful and fun.

And this seemed almost fun to the girl, like an experience that was improving the way Mr. Earl looked in her eyes. He sat her down on the couch and stood in front of the television, opened the tape and slid it into the VCR. Navi finally got a glimpse of the cover of the movie and she was relieved to see a pretty blonde lady in a flowing pink dress, which made her think this movie probably had a princess in it. Navi loved stories about princesses.

As the movie started to play and Mr. Earl came and sat next to her on the couch, Navi suddenly felt the unmistakable presence of the Father with her once again.

"Hello Navi, my beautiful princess!" He exclaimed over her.

"Hello Father! I am so glad to see you today! I'm going to watch a movie about a real princess with Mr. Earl." she replied.

"Ah, yes, I know he is showing you a movie today. That is why I have come to you. You are right to say this movie is about a real life princess, but Navi, she does not know that about herself. Her heart is sad and her life is broken and I desperately want to share my love with her like I am sharing it with you."

Navi knew that every word the Father was saying to her was true. She could feel the love He had for her flowing out of Him and saturating her, covering her like a blanket. She realized that Mr. Earl had spread an actual blanket over their laps, but the blanket from her Father felt even more real than that one.

"Navi, I want you to see the princess in this movie the way I see her," the Father said. "I want to give you My love for all people, so you will always see the very best in them."

"That sounds wonderful Father!" Navi chirped back.

"Someday you will radiate My love to everyone around you, just like I am doing right now," He said.

Navi cooed when she heard that. The warm sensations of the Father's love were tickling her whole body, from her head to her toes.

"Until then I need you to be My strong and brave Princess Navi. Can you do that? Can you be strong and brave no matter what happens?" He asked.

"Yes Father, I will always do whatever You ask me. Your love is so good I can feel it!" the child answered.

"You are one of my favorites, Princess Navi!" the Father declared over her.

Navi smiled widely as she snuggled her head down on the couch and pulled the blanket up around her shoulders. She was so serene after all of the kind words that had been spoken and was lingering in the glow of the Father's love all over her.

It was true that the movie Mr. Earl showed her had a princess in it, and she found a prince and kissed him, too. There were many confusing and even scary things that happened while she watched it, but Navi stayed brave in spite of the fear.

When the movie was over Mr. Earl put it back in the case and told Navi he was going to take a shower. He put her favorite cartoon back on and left the room, and just a few minutes later her little sister came in and climbed up on the couch to watch it with her.

After such a strange afternoon Navi had a bellyache. She made her little sister a peanut butter sandwich and before Mr. Earl got out of the shower she and her little sister went to their room to play with their dolls, closing their door tightly behind them. They both decided to lay down on their makeshift bed earlier than usual that evening and they both had a fitful night of sleep.

They woke the next morning to the shouts and slams of the mom and Mr. Earl having an intense argument. There were obviously things being thrown and broken and the mom was sobbing loudly.

With the door shut the girls couldn't understand most of what the adults were yelling at each other, but somehow Navi knew it all had something to do with the movies in the top of their closet.

[9]
THE FINER THINGS IN LIFE

THE NEXT SEVERAL WEEKS OF NAVI'S LIFE WERE FILLED with watching the movies from the closet and looking at pictures in magazines. It was like clockwork - every day when her little sister would take her afternoon nap, Mr. Earl would bring out a video to watch with Navi or he would open a glossy magazine filled with pictures of pretty women wearing lots of makeup and not many clothes, posing like models in fancy places.

Every time they sat on the couch together, Mr. Earl would be just a little more brazen than the time before. He would say things to Navi about how good the people in the movies felt or how beautiful the women in the magazines looked. He would ask Navi if she liked to feel good and look beautiful. He told her that she could be like these pretty women and he could take pictures of her being pretty like these magazine ladies. He told her there were lots of men who would like to make her feel good like the movie star women. And every time he put the videotapes and magazines away he would remind Navi that this was a special secret time he was spending with her and if she didn't tell anyone about what they did one day she would get to be in movies and magazines too.

Navi was really starting to feel differently about Mr. Earl. She was happy that he thought she was special and she even started looking forward to the time they would spend together each afternoon. This was a time of deep bonding for them.

As the weeks passed Mr. Earl's office did call and Navi was enrolled in school. He was going to work in a suit everyday and Navi was headed to Kindergarten each morning. The mom and little sister stayed home all day and the mom only worked about half as much after a while.

Life was seemingly normal and in the evenings and on the weekends Navi and her little sister would play outside with some of the kids their age who lived in the apartment complex. The mild weather in their South Texas town made it easy to spend time outdoors even as the year was coming to an end.

Before long, Christmas arrived and Navi and her little sister got to wake up to a big surprise that morning - there were presents for each of them wrapped up under the tree! As the girls excitedly tore open each one the mom made two piles on the floor. Little sister's pile had socks, new pajamas, some books, cartoon themed games and toys and a cute, fluffy teddy bear. Navi's pile had socks, a new dress, some books and a little makeup kit, a toy camera and a beautiful babydoll in a pink dress. Each girl also had the pleasure of dumping out a little stocking full of candy and fruit.

After all the excitement of ripping into the presents started wearing off the mom and Mr. Earl sat on the couch sipping coffee as the girls played with their new toys and ate their candies. There was an amazing peace and a sense of normalcy that just rested in the room.

Navi picked up her beautiful babydoll and ran the little plastic brush that came with her through the long blond curls that crowned her head. She looked up at Mr. Earl and said, "I'm going to name her after that pretty princess in our movie! Doesn't she look just like her?"

That comment was all it took to split the facade of harmony in the house right in half. The mom's face turned bright red with anger and Mr. Earl's face turned pale white with shock. He looked like he had been punched in the stomach and the mom looked like she was about to punch him in the stomach.

Slamming down her coffee cup, she stood up and marched to their bedroom, slamming the door behind her so hard a vase fell off of a shelf and busted on the floor.

Mr. Earl spat through his clenched teeth, "Navi, that is our special secret!" as he hurried into the bedroom, chasing after the mom with his tail between his legs. As soon as the door shut behind him there was an eruption of screaming and shouting and slamming.

There had been so many times of conflict explosions in this little apartment that Navi's little sister was hardly fazed this time. She just went on playing with her new toy and singing her little song.

Navi, however, was not so happy go lucky. She realized that she had done something to break the trust Mr. Earl had built with her and that made her feel like there was a knot being tied way deep down in her tummy. She didn't want to disappoint him and she decided right then that as soon as she was able to she would make it up to him.

Within just a few minutes the yelling and fighting settled down and before long the adults emerged from their room. The mom walked over to the table and dried up her spilled coffee with a little towel and carried her cup off to put it in the sink in the tiny kitchen. Mr. Earl sat back down in his spot on the couch and flipped on the television. An old movie about Christmas was playing and just having the background noise seemed to calm the room ever so slightly.

When the mom came back in the room she sat down on the couch next to Mr. Earl and lit one of her long, brown cigarettes. She seemed to look anywhere but at Navi and allowed her eyes to settle on the boring movie playing quietly on the tv set. As she sat there with her blank stare and took long, slow drags off of the cigarette, Mr. Earl reached down in the couch cushions and pulled out an especially sparkly box and sheepishly handed it to the mom.

"Merry Christmas, Baby," he whispered to her.

The mom's face instantly softened as she took the gift and slid the ribbon off. She said a customary, "Oh, honey, you shouldn't have," and opened the lid to reveal a beautiful necklace.

"It's perfect!" she exclaimed as she lifted the hair from the back of her neck so Mr. Earl could fasten it on her.

Navi didn't understand what was going on inside of her as she watched him put the strand of pearls around the mom's neck but she felt such a strong sense of jealousy and competition.

She turned from the adults and started playing her own little game with her little porn-star-look-alike baby doll. Pretending the beautiful doll was a princess she flipped her hair around and spun her skirt as she crafted a tale of all the men in the countryside bringing her gifts and telling her how perfect and beautiful she was.

The awkward family Christmas stretched throughout the day and included a phone call with the grandmom and granddad and a big dinner at the dining table, served on real plates with mashed potatoes and warm bread.

By the time evening rolled around the little girls were ready to go to their room and fall asleep. As they started rubbing their eyes and getting listless the mom asked them if they were ready for bed and they both nodded their sleepy little heads. The mom motioned at Mr. Earl and the adults excitedly led them down the hallway to their bedroom and proudly threw open the door.

The little girls were shocked and surprised to see a beautiful pink princess canopy bed and dresser radiantly shimmering in their tiny bedroom. They rushed to the bed and climbed up on it, jumping up and down on the gauzy pink ruffled comforter as they giggled with pure joy.

"Girls, we wanted you to have a special bed in your room. This one is made for real princesses, so we knew it was perfect for you!" Mr. Earl proudly declared.

"This will be your own special place, girls. We want you to have sweet dreams as you lay in this bed every night," the mom added.

"Thank you! Thank you! Thank you!" the girls chorused.

They were nearly too excited to sleep, but as their bounces slowed and their giggles quieted they found their way beneath the covers of their gleaming new bed and rested their heads on their puffy pink pillows as they drifted off to dream princess dreams.

THE FATHER VISITED Navi that night in her dreams. It was a special time of Him revealing His great love to her and affirming her as His child, truly a real-life princess. He reminded her to be strong and brave and before the dream was over He made a promise to her that the special new bed she and her sister shared would be a place that was off limits to Mr. Earl and his strange requests. The Father assured Navi that just like she could see the canopy over top of it this new bed would be covered with angels and they would keep it a pure and undefiled place.

Navi and her little sister woke from the best night ever to a new day filled with new gifts and games. They played like children do, creating their own storylines and adventures with their toys and dolls. They could have stayed in their room playing all day long, but close to lunchtime the mom came in to check on them. She had yet another surprise for them and opened the door to their closet to showed them two sparkly dresses covered with sequins.

The mom announced to the girls they were going to a fancy party at a fancy place this evening and they were going to wear their fancy dresses and have their hair fixed up and wear their little patent leather shoes. The girls were so excited and they could hardly contain themselves all day as they waited for their fancy princess party.

As the time passed the girls had a long bath and they were dressed in their pretty dresses. Their hair was pulled up and their little white ruffled socks and patent leather shoes were slipped on. Once they were all ready the mom sat them on the couch with explicit instructions not to mess up their hair or clothes. She put one of their cartoon movies in the VCR and she and Mr. Earl went into their bedroom. When they came out the girls were amazed to see how glamorous they looked.

Mr. Earl had on a fancy suit with a black bow tie and the mom wore a glimmering gown with her hair curled and the strand of pearls shining around her neck. The mom really looked like a movie star with her pretty makeup and red fingernails. Navi and her little sister were so proud and excited to go with them to the fancy party.

They all walked out of their apartment and climbed into the car. The whole drive to the party the mom was giving instructions to the little girls.

"Now remember, girls, children are to be seen and not heard, so I do not want you whining, complaining or speaking at all unless you are spoken to first by an adult."

"You must mind your manners and always keep yourselves clean and neat, do not spill anything on your dresses or make any messes."

"This is a country club, so remember no running, no shouting and no horseplay."

"Navi, you will be going with Mr. Earl so he can introduce you to some important people and your little sister will either stay with me or go to the children's area."

"Girls, I will tell you this only once - when I say it is time to leave we are going to leave, not a minute before or a moment after. I don't want to hear any whining that you're bored and want to go or any fits that you want to stay and play with your new friends."

"Okay, we are here, remember everything I told you and be good girls on your very best behavior!" she added as they pulled into the parking lot.

Mr Earl pulled up in front of the opulent building and men opened the doors for the family to exit the car. A man sat in the drivers seat and drove off in their car as another man rushed to open the big, ornate door for them to enter through. The place was electric with music and chatter and before they even got their bearings a photographer with a big camera stopped them to capture a family photo in front of a giant lavishly decorated Christmas tree.

The mom posed the girls and then herself and Mr. Earl beamed as the picture was snapped. Everyone was glowing and bright with cheesy smiles spread across their faces. Once their eyes adjusted from the big flashbulbs going off they went from the entryway into the ballroom.

This elegant room was decorated from floor to ceiling and everyone was dressed in fancy party suits and long, sparkling gowns. As they made their way across the room to the punch bowl the adults were handed tall, thin glasses of champagne and little hors d'oeuvres on embellished napkins. When they reached the table with the tiny glass cups and big bowl of sparkling red punch the mom smiled at the server and said, "Two, please."

She daintily handed the girls the petite cups and reminded them not to spill. The girls carefully sipped the crimson juice as they watched Mr. Earl speak to a business associate who had stopped to exchange pleasantries. He tugged on the mom's elbow to spin her around to face the man and his lovely wife.

"This is my better half. Better looking, for one!" Mr. Earl joked as the adults all broke into cackles of laughter. They introduced one another and the men shook hands with the ladies and the ladies kissed one another lightly on the cheeks. Then, the man bent down so he was eye level with the little girls.

"You must be Navi," he said, looking the six year old in the eyes quizzically.

"Yes, sir, I am," she answered, remembering the mom's instruction about being polite to the adults.

"Well, I have heard quite a lot about you, little girl. I am so happy you were able to come along tonite. Has Mr. Earl shown you to the sitting room?" he asked her.

"No sir," she answered as she shook her head.

"Well, what are we waiting for! Come, Mr. Earl, let's show her the special sitting room. Honey, please show our new friend where she can take her little girl to play with the other children and we will meet you ladies back in here shortly for some more champagne and dancing." the new man instructed his wife.

"Of course, darling," she replied as she kissed his cheek

and took the mom and little sister by the hand to lead them back across the crowded room.

"Come on, Navi, I have something very special to show you," Mr. Earl smiled. He and the new man led Navi into the hallway just off of the big ballroom.

The door opened into the men's bathroom and Navi was surprised to see men standing at the urinals, but she was quickly escorted past them and through another doorway. The next room had hallways off each side with rows of lockers and long wooden benches running down the middle of them. As they passed the rows of lockers they walked by booths of shower stalls and finally through another doorway into a new room.

"This must be the Sitting Room," Navi thought to herself, because it was filled with a lot of little couches and padded chaise lounges. There were about a dozen men in the room and several young girls Navi's age or a little older. Everyone was dressed in their party clothes and they seemed to be happy and having fun.

The lights were a bit dimmer than they had been in the restroom and the locker room, and this room felt warm and comfortable. It was well decorated with flower arrangements and fancy adornments on the big wooden tables and lots of overstuffed pillows and soft throw blankets placed throughout the room.

Navi saw there were some televisions around the room and they all seemed to have their own VCR which were playing movies that were very similar to the ones Mr. Earl would show her at home, but these movies all seemed to have only men and girls like her, instead of men with grown women.

As the men led Navi to one of the couches her heart started beating faster and that familiar lump rose up in her throat. She looked closer to the other men and little girls around the room and she realized they were all doing things like what was being shown on the movies. Navi got very nervous and started to push Mr. Earl and his friend away, but they coaxed her and spoke softly to calm her down.

Mr. Earl gave her a big drink from a glass of punch that was on the table next to them and as Navi swallowed the sweet and sour juice she started to feel a little tingle through her hands and feet.

"Here, Navi, have some more," he suggested as he gave her another gulp.

That helped her to stop resisting them and her nervousness melted away. As she sat on the couch with them she became more comfortable and relaxed and started to crave the attention the men were pouring over her.

When their time was over in the sitting room and they walked past the lockers and through the restroom, Navi heard the new man telling Mr. Earl what a good job she had done.

"I'll be sure to recommend that promotion for you at the

start of the new year," he said firmly, a glint in his eye as he winked at Mr. Earl.

When they reentered the ballroom and found their dates they excitedly toasted champagne and took turns leading them up to the dance floor as one of the couples sat at the table with Navi. As the evening came to an end and the mom went to get her little sister from the children's area, both of the girls had drifted off to sleep and needed carried out to the car.

The mom and Mr. Earl chattered the whole way home and discussed their big plans to get a new car and a new house once he was promoted and he started making more money. It really seemed as if finally everything was working out the way it had been planned and they would be able to start enjoying the finer things in life.

[10]

GATHERINGS

OVER THE NEXT FEW YEARS ALL OF THE MOM'S DREAMS really were coming true. Once Mr. Earl was promoted at the bank where he worked they were finally able to move out of the tiny, cramped apartment and have a new home built in one of the most up-and-coming areas of their city. They traded their beat-up car for two new ones: a Cadillac for Mr. Earl to drive to and from work everyday and a fast, sporty car for the mom to drive to the nightclub where she worked. There seemed to be new furniture delivered every few months and the house started to fill up with the newest electronics, the fanciest decorations and the finest luxuries.

Their new house was in the perfect neighborhood. It was walking distance to the water and to the girls' schools. Since they lived in a semi-tropical climate, most days Navi would walk her little sister to her school building and then go to the next building over to her own classes. It was really convenient when school let out too, because the little sister would wait for Navi to come get her so they could walk home together. Sometimes the mom would already be gone and Mr. Earl would always work during the day, so the girls often walked home to an empty house, but they knew not to answer the door or the phone and to do their homework, have a snack and watch television until one of the grown-ups came home. Even though Navi was only nine years old she was very mature for her age and she did a good job babysitting her little sister.

Since Mr. Earl had such a great job once he had received the promotion at work, the mom only worked when she wanted to now instead of working because she had to. She was so happy to only work a few nights a week. During the days she spent a lot of her time laying in the sun by the pool so she would have a nice tan and she often had her nails and hair done. She needed to always look her best at the club so she would shop for sexy new clothes and high-end makeup and perfumes. On most nights when she wasn't working at the club she would go out to party with her girlfriends to dance and drink and have fun. Many nights she don't get home till after midnight and the times when Navi saw her come in she knew she was drunk or high by the way she looked and acted.

Sometimes Mr. Earl would take the mom to work in his Cadillac and he would drop her off at the front of the club.

Navi and her little sister would be in the backseat and they would wave goodbye and blow kisses to the mom as she walked through the door into the smoky, dark club. When they left the parking lot they always drove under the big, flashing neon outline of a lady laying on her back with her legs up in the air and Navi would imagine the mom laying like that while men threw money at her like she had seen in the movies she and Mr. Earl would watch with his friends.

Nearly every night when the mom was working or out with her friends Mr. Earl would have Navi tuck her little sister into their pink princess canopy bed and then she would come back out into the living room where Mr. Earl was waiting for her. They had a little routine and Navi knew what to expect nearly every night. First, she would go over to the little bar in the corner of the room and make Mr. Earl his whiskey drink and if he had another gentleman with him she would ask him what he would like to drink and serve him as well. The men were always impressed that Navi could make their drinks and serve them with little swizzle sticks and cocktail napkins. Sometimes Navi would have a little fruity drink with them and that would help her to relax and seemed to take the lump out of her throat.

Mr. Earl and his friends always seemed to want the same things. Either they would have her do a little fashion show wearing the mom's dancing clothes, which were really just like sexy costumes, and then they would have Navi come sit on the couch with them as they enacted the scenes from the movies that were always playing on the television, or they would have Mr. Earl take Navi to the master bedroom where he would give her very specific instructions of what to do when his friend came in the room. Most of the things she had to do were pretty easy and she had watched it done on the movies hundreds of times, but sometimes the men would try to do things that Mr. Earl hadn't told her about so she would have to ring a little bell on the nightstand.

If she rang that bell Mr. Earl would come in the room and firmly tell his friend to get dressed and leave. They always acted like they had gotten in trouble and Navi never saw those men again. It seemed like the only men Mr. Earl wanted to bring around were the ones who were really kind and gentle and they usually even acted a little nervous and scared. That helped Navi feel at ease since they were almost always really nice to her.

A lot of the men would bring her presents like candy and teddy bears and dresses. She loved all the attention she would get, especially when they would do a photoshoot of Navi in the little dancing costumes or one of the men would bring a fancy camera to make a movie just like the ones Mr. Earl always showed her. The photos they took of her got printed out and shared and Navi was so proud to know Mr. Earl had all of his favorites in a special album he kept on his desk at work. When she would go to his office she would look through the album at all her pretty pictures and sometimes when Mr. Earl would introduce her to some of the men he worked with they would tell her she was even prettier than in her pictures.

As they made more and more movies Navi would beam proudly as Mr. Earl would put the new tape up in he and the mom's closet. The movie collection had grown from only about a dozen of them in the beginning to eventually stretching nearly the entire length of the top shelf of the walk-in closet. Navi felt like a real movie star knowing her tapes were up there in the same place as the ones with the pretty blonde princess who she had named her Christmas doll after a few years earlier.

Some of the men who would come to see Navi had daughters her age and sometimes they would bring them along. Navi and the other girls would do the fashion shows and it was always fun for her to see them watch her movies and learn how to do all the things Mr. Earl and his friends wanted to do. She liked being their teacher and helping them learn how to dance or act pretty for the cameras. If the other girls were nervous or scared Navi could always help them calm down by making them a yummy fruity drink. And if Navi ever spent the night with these friends sometimes their daddies would have the girls play dress up and other games for them at their houses too.

This life seemed to be going along so well. Navi and her little sister were doing great in school, the mom was always the star of the show at her nightclub and had lots of beautiful friends to go out with at night and Mr. Earl was doing great at his job with the bank. He had impressed many of the men by bringing Navi to entertain them at the yacht clubs and country clubs or the fancy parties in their big, lavish mansions. The more impressed the men were, the more money Mr. Earl would end up making or the better title he would receive at work. One of the men even came up with a special deal for Mr. Earl to get him involved in real estate so he could make even more money and meet even more influential people.

One day, however, things got a little complicated. Mr. Earl had tried something new with Navi where he had her get on the bed and he laid on top of her. When he was finished they realized she was bleeding and he got very angry at her because she had made a mess on the mom's side of the bed. He yelled at her and told her to clean it up and get the sheets into the laundry right away. Navi was crying because she was scared and she knew that she had upset him. The bleeding kind of hurt her too, so she was very worried that she would be in a lot of trouble over this whole situation.

As she stood in front of the washing machine trying to scrub the blood from the sheets the Father suddenly appeared to her. Navi was so glad to see Him and just His presence coming near made her tears instantly dry up.

"Hello, Navi," He said with His rich, deep words. She

loved hearing Him say that because when He said her name He always made it sound like a song.

"Hello Father, I am so glad you are here," Navi replied, genuinely happy and filled with joy.

"You've done so well being my strong and brave princess, Navi. I am so proud of you," He said to her in His heavy voice. When He released those words they seemed to cling to the atmosphere with a thickness. The Father pulled her close to Himself and hid her under the shadow of His wing. He wanted to let her see things the way He saw them and see herself free from Mr. Earl and his friends so she could have hope to endure.

"Navi, things will not be like this forever. You are going to be free someday and because of that freedom you are going to gather many, many of My daughters back to Me," He told her.

"When Mr. Earl and his friends do these things to you I cry and mourn," He told her. "Not because I am sad for you, though, Navi. I know you are connected to me, and I know you will one day live your life with Me and fulfill the purpose and destiny I created you for! But I cry for these men," He said.

"I cry because every time they use you to go deeper into their world of sin they take themselves farther from Me. I cry because they are blinded by their own lusts and the love of money that is dragging them to the pit of hell. I cry because they are hurting themselves more than they could ever hurt you. You are covered with My grace, but they pull away from Me more and more everyday. I cry because they will be separated from Me forever and I long to see them come to an end of the destructive patterns of sin they are creating."

He looked Navi deep in the eyes, "These men are not who I am, Navi. Their love is only for themselves and their sinful hearts have destroyed their ability to connect with Me or you or anyone else," He told her. "

They are creating the only world they will ever know - a world where sin breeds death and lust leaves them empty. The nightmare of their lives will be fulfilled on the day they stand before Me and I ask them for an account of their lives. Then they will eternally be separated from Me and have no opportunity for redemption.

"But you, Navi, your story is different!" He said with light bursting from His eyes.

"You are my brave princess and inside of you is the heart of a warrior! No evil thing can ever destroy you and one day you will completely triumph over every bad thing that has ever been done to you. When that day comes, you will work with Me to forcefully advance My Kingdom in the lives of so many people throughout the world. Your story of victory is going to be an arrow that will point many others to Me so they can be set free."

"Father, I want to work with You, I want to build Your Kingdom!" Navi agreed.

"My child, be assured that the time will come! Until then continue to be brave and never forget about My great love for you!" He proclaimed over her.

This encounter was enough to keep Navi encouraged and gave her so much strength to endure. She never discussed these precious times with the Father with anyone else, but she relished each time they happened over the next few years. Every encounter seemed stronger than the last and each time she gathered more courage than the time before.

Some hide, terrified the OTHERS
will find them.

[11]
REJECTION & ACCEPTANCE

Navi was growing up. Her body had developed early compared to the other girls in her class at school and some of the mean girls in her class were quick to point that out. It seemed like everyday Navi was being rejected by a new group of her peers, in spite of her concentrated efforts to the contrary.

It didn't matter how the other kids treated her or what was happening at home, Navi always worked hard on her schoolwork and took her studies seriously. She tested to the highest in her class on every test the schools administered and she was always in the top of her gifted and talented class. The teachers had always appreciated Navi finishing her assignments early and helping them with the other students. She was always so eager to please others, especially adults in positions of authority.

Up until junior high school she had always gotten along with everyone in her class and even had kids older than her and younger than her who she counted as friends. She always made it a point to have at least a couple allies in her little sister's class so she wouldn't have to worry about her being picked on or bullied. It seemed as if the kids three years behind her knew there was a big sister who might come hunt them down they would forgo the usual teasing and hazing.

Seventh graders can be especially cruel, and Navi was quickly becoming the butt of jokes for everyone in her class. When the cool, rich kids rejected her she just brushed it off because they were always fickle and she figured she would just fit in with the nerdy smart kids. After all, she was smart and had a wit to match because most of her conversations in her daily life were with wealthy adults in country club settings. But because Navi was a bit ignorant about pre-teen matters and she couldn't relate to the nerdy kids on a life experience level, they quickly made it obvious she wasn't a part of their crowd either.

Navi didn't have an athletic bone in her body, but in desperation to fit in somewhere she joined the dance and cheer team. As she went to the practices and had to change clothes in front of the other girls in the locker room she began to realize maybe that was a mistake, too. She was already quite a bit taller and curvier than the other girls, with thick hips and thighs. Her bra hadn't been a training size in more than two years and she was wearing clothes and shoes from the adult ladies section of the stores, not the little girls and preteens. She had already been having her period and wearing deodorant for a couple of years and she had been shaving her legs and under her arms for almost as long.

The locker room chatter always made Navi extremely uncomfortable. She would hear the mean girls say things like, "Look at her, she has boobs as big as my mom's!" or "I can smell her stinky sweat, she needs to shower!" and it always cut her to the bone. She decided the only way to combat the incessant teasing was for her to work harder than any of the other girls and learn the dance routine for their halftime football performance absolutely perfectly.

As Navi worked harder on that dance routine she became a little more withdrawn from the things that were happening at her house. She realized that there were other boys and girls just a year ahead of her who were doing similar things as what she would see in the movies or do with Mr. Earl and his friends, but they were doing it with other eighth graders, not with people their parents' ages. That put a new layer of complexity on Navi and it made it harder to fulfill the expectations of the men as well. In a strange way, things were changing in the way they treated her because she was developing and looked more like a woman. For some of them it was even more attractive, but for others it seemed to cause them to lose interest.

Navi was really having a sort of crisis. The best thing she always had going for her was the attention of men, with them telling her how pretty she was and how much she impressed them. With that attention hit or miss at this time in her life, she couldn't get her self esteem boosted by them any longer. Her school performance had always earned her attention and after bringing home all A's on every report card she had ever received this year she was distracted and not giving her studies the attention they deserved. It showed on her first review and she had B's and even some C's in some classes.

Even at home with her little sister Navi was becoming detached. When they would get home from school she would immediately go to their bedroom or into the backyard to practice the dance moves for the halftime show. If she messed up a step or got out of rhythm she would become so disappointed in herself and feel helpless and worthless. Her confidence seemed to lack more with each passing day.

Navi had started to make herself a fruity drink from the bar when she made her little sister an after school snack. It was becoming familiar to her to have the tingling feeling in her hands and feet instead of the nervousness in her head and chest. She had also made some friends from the eighth and ninth grades who were doing more than just drinking, they were also smoking cigarettes and some of them were even smoking pot.

One day when the girls came home after school the

mom was at the house. She obviously didn't feel well and looked as if she had been sleeping all day and had just woken up when she had heard the girls coming in the door. She told Navi she had a bad headache and gave her a note and some money to take down to the convenience store to get some cigarettes and a can of soda to kill her hangover. It was not normal for a convenience store to send a young girl home with her mom's cigarettes, no matter what the note said, but the man running this particular store never cared how old his customers were. Kids not much older than Navi bought packs of smokes there nearly everyday when school let out and they would often stand behind the building and smoke them with all their friends.

When Navi got to the little shop she saw four of those bad kids hanging out, doing tricks on their skateboards in the parking lot. She tried to ignore them but also didn't want to seem rude or stuck up. Actually, what was heaviest on her mind was quickly running this errand for the mom so she could get home and practice her dance.

"Hey Navi, whatcha doin?" one of the cute ninth graders mumbled at her.

Navi was absolutely taken aback that the good-looking young man knew her name and who she was. It caused her to stop her stride and drop her hand from pushing the shop door open.

"I'm getting something for my mother. What are you doing?" she chided back.

"We were gonna go smoke one, you wanna come along?" he asked her, his eyes playful in spite of the shy grin on his face.

"Sure, just let me grab this stuff for her, I'll be right out," Navi replied as she turned to enter the store.

She was so shocked that she had just been invited to hang out with that really cute older boy and his friends, she hadn't even given much thought to what he was intending to smoke. In Navi's still innocent mind they were going to smoke one of the long nasty brown cigarettes like she was picking up for the mom. She didn't really want to smoke one of those, but if it meant a little attention and time spent with that cute older boy, she was willing to do it.

She grabbed the bag from the store clerk and hurried out the door. The cute boy and his friends had waited for her and once she joined them in the parking lot they stopped doing their skateboard tricks and gathered around her. The cute boy asked, "Are you ready to smoke, Navi?"

She replied a curt, "Yeah, let's go," as if it was a daily thing she did, smoking.

That was all it took to encourage the cute boy to lead the little group to the alleyway behind the store. Once they all gathered back there behind the dumpster he dug in his shirt pocket and proudly pulled out a lumpy, long little wad of paper that didn't at all resemble the brown cigarettes the mom smoked.

"Who's got a light?" he asked as he stuffed the fat end in his mouth.

One of his friends sparked a lighter and set the long, pointy cigarette on fire. After the cute boy took a couple puffs off of it he passed it to his buddy. As it went around the circle Navi quickly became aware this wasn't a regular cigarette they were sharing, it smelled like a skunk and made the four boys choke and gag, but they all laughed about it like it was great fun to cough up a lung. When the burning joint was finally passed to Navi she wasn't sure what to do with it. The cute boy sensed her anxiety and he helped her. As he held it for her to keep her fingers from getting burnt he coached her on how to puff on it and hold in her smoke. Navi coughed and gagged too, but since everyone else was as well it didn't seem like a big deal.

The stinky joint only made it around the circle for everyone to puff on it twice and that was all it took for Navi. Her hands and feet went numb much like that first fruity drink would make her feel, but as she leaned her body back on the wall she realized this feeling was a hundred times the intensity of even two or three of those drinks. She really didn't have a care in the world and actually let the bag she had been holding with the mom's soda and cigarettes fall to the ground.

All the guys in the alley were laughing, but Navi didn't think they were necessarily laughing at her, just laughing at everything in general. She felt like she was stuck to the ground but like she could just float away at the same time. Her head was spinning and she could feel her heart pounding slowly in her chest, beating harder with each deep breath she took.

"You like this feeling, don't you girl," the cute boy asked her as he slipped his mouth over hers in a crude attempt at a kiss as his hand reached up her shirt to grab a handful of her breast.

Navi felt too good to be scared but the cackling of the three other boys snapped her out of her haze. She tried to pull away from the cute boy and push him off of her and when she got her mouth away from his she used all the breath she had in her lungs to push out the word "NO" as loud as she could. Her struggles to stop the cute boy seemed to get the other boys even more stirred up and she suddenly felt both of the cute boys hands up her shirt, one grabbing each breast.

Navi saw a glimmer of hope to get away from these boys and she raised her knee to the cute boy's groin and pushed him away. As he stumbled backwards she stooped down to retrieve the mom's care package and bolted around to the front of the shop. The further she got from the crowd of boys the less cloudy her mind was and she finally decided to take off running to get back home.

It took Navi less than ten minutes to get to her house and she hadn't even stopped to check behind her to see if she was being followed, she just kept running. When she finally got to her front door she busted in and quickly slammed the door shut, locking it behind her. The mom was obviously agitated because Navi had taken so long to bring back her things and she complained about the cigarettes being crumpled and the soda can being dented.

Navi was too high to let the mom's complaints faze her and she just headed past her sister watching cartoons in the living room and went straight to her room where she collapsed face down on the princess canopy bed. She had never been so tired and she fell asleep fast and hard.

[12]
CALLED OUT

Navi slept right through dinner and clear until the next morning. When she woke up for school she felt like her head had been hit with a hammer but she did everything she could to get her stuff together to get out the door for school. The final rehearsal for the dance team halftime show would be held right after lunch today. Since the day before had been the worst Monday ever and she wasn't able to practice, she had been going over the song and the steps all morning long.

Once she was settled into her morning class she heard a familiar sound over the loudspeaker. It was the principal's assistant making the daily announcements, and she finished by calling one of the bad kids to the office. Navi tried to block it out and keep counting off the dance steps in her head: five, six, seven, eight; but her teacher came and tapped on her desk to bring her back from her daydream.

"Navi, you're being called to the office," the teacher said, looking at her seriously.

Instantly feeling her face get bright red she slowly stood up as all the students snickered their oooh's and aaah's. She bolted out of the door, trying to figure out what rules she had broken to be called to the principal's office. She wondered if the principal had found out that she had smoked behind the little shop with those older boys the day before. She wondered if she was in trouble because that cute ninth grade boy had put his hands up her shirt. The whole way to the principal's office her mind was racing with wondering why.

When Navi finally did get to the office the answer to her whys was almost scarier than her imaginations in the hallway. When she came into the room she saw two big policemen and it was obvious they were waiting for her.

"Hello Navi," the two officers said in unison as they quickly introduced themselves.

"We need to take you downtown to talk with you," one of them said to her very matter-of-factly.

Before Navi really knew what was happening the two men in uniforms led her out to the squad car they had parked in front of the school building and had her climb into the backseat. Navi was really concerned now because she knew only criminals rode in the backs of police cars.

The men tried to keep the conversation light along the ride and Navi tried to keep her tears at bay.

The officer riding in the passenger seat turned toward her and asked, "Do you know what this is about? Mr. Earl and Mr. Smith?"

"No, what about them?" Navi replied.

"Well, one of your little friends told a teacher that Mr. Earl tried to touch her privates and she said that you had told her that he and Mr. Smith had tried to touch yours too," the cop stated matter of factly as he snapped the gum in his mouth.

Navi felt the bottom fall out of her stomach. Mr. Earl had warned her of what would happen if anyone besides the men he shared Navi with ever found out about their special times together. He had been very specific of what to say and what not to say if the police ever asked her about all of the things they did together. He warned her that she could get taken away and sent to jail for a very long time and she wouldn't be allowed to see the mom, him or her little sister again.

Navi chose to ride the rest of the way in silence. Once they arrived at the police station they parked the patrol car in the garage and led her into a big room. It was filled with lots of other police officers sitting at desks making phone calls and other people who obviously were not police scattered throughout the room. Some of them looked mean and angry and one of them even growled at the officer Navi was following.

She was ushered into a little room and the officers started asking her some questions. They said strange things like, "Did Mr. Earl ever try to touch your privates?" and "Did Mr. Smith touch you in a private place?" Navi tried her best to give the answers she had been told to give from Mr. Earl but she got a couple of them mixed up a little bit. She was quickly frustrated with the police and that was quite obvious to them. They finally left her alone in the room for what seemed like an eternity.

Navi was very anxious about how long they had been away from the school and she was concerned she was missing her dance team's practice. She knew attending this afternoon's final dress rehearsal was a requirement for participating in the halftime show on Thursday, so more than anything she wanted this to be over with so these cops would take her back to her school. There was so much pressure mounting on the little girl and she felt as if she was about to break.

When Navi thought she couldn't bear another minute of waiting and she was just about to try and open the door to the stark little room she had been left in, the door suddenly opened and the same two bumble-headed officers came in and sat across the table from her.

"Alrighty, young lady, we are gonna need you to sign off on this paperwork. And, just so you know, we don't want you talking about coming down here today with anyone, not your mother, your little friends at school or anyone else, understand?" one of them rattled off matter of factly.

"Oh, and by the way, because you're signing off on this now, we can promise that you won't ever have to appear in court or have any other interviews or encounters with people from children's services," the other officer added, smacking his gum the whole time he talked.

"Well, I guess so. What do you need me to sign? Are you going to take me back to the school now?" Navi asked, not even attempting to mask her desperation.

"Here ya go," said the gum snapper as he spun a piece of paper around on the table so Navi could read it. "Just sign there at the bottom," he instructed.

Navi took the pen he was handing her and almost signed the page so she could get out of this little room and back to her school and back to the practice, but she stopped cold when she took a closer look at what was written on the paper.

'My name is Navi. I am twelve years old. I live at blah, blah, blah. Mr. Earl tried to touch my privates. Mr. Smith told me he wanted to touch me on my privates.' And on and on the narrative went, sounding like an uneducated little child had answered a list of fill in the blank questions.

Navi thought, "Surely I didn't sound this ignorant to the officers, did I?"

"I can't sign this, I didn't say these things. You made it sound like I am some stupid little kid who doesn't have a good vocabulary, and I always get good grades in my language class." Navi protested, adding, "Plus, it says down here that by signing it that 'I confirm no law enforcement officer has made any promises or coerced me in any way' and you just told me you promised that I would never go to court and all those other things!"

The officers were stunned when they heard the little girl's arguments. In their minds she was acting a little too smart for her own good. The gum snapper quickly retorted, trying to tell her those rules didn't apply to her because she was a minor and they hadn't really made any promises about court. But not to worry, he said, signing this form would assure that she never had to attend any of the court proceedings. At this point the child couldn't decide if these cops were stupid or if they just thought that she was.

As time melted away, Navi knew her chances of making it to her practice were getting slimmer. In total despair she scribbled her name on the bottom of the form and looked up at the faces of her two captors asking, "Can we go now?"

Much to her surprise, with that one simple question, the men both started gathering papers and preparing to leave the little room where they had been holding her. She had no idea of the time of day or any concept of how long they had been in the building but Navi was hoping with all she had within herself that she would make it to her practice on time.

"Five, six, seven, eight," she counted in her head as she waited for the men to release her. She went over every step, every movement of her routine and fantasized performing in front of the crowd that would be gathering in the stands two days from then.

After what seemed like hours of waiting, the men finally returned to retrieve the girl. They led her through the big room filled with cops and criminals and then down the long hallway to the elevator. As they led her from the elevator to their squad car Navi was still mentally reviewing the moves to her dance.

They had the girl sit in the backseat again and once she was secured the driver pulled out of the parking garage and began ambling down the road. The group rode back to the school in complete silence and when they finally pulled up in front of the building Navi couldn't exit the vehicle fast enough.

Once she was released from the supervision of the officers she bolted through the door and ran straight into the principal's office. As she burst into the room she was shocked to see the clock silently declaring the time to be 3:15 in the afternoon. Navi knew that meant the dance team practice was over and she had missed her chance to rehearse with the team. Her heart dropped to the ground. In a flash of tears she ran out of the office and right through the school, crossed the street and kept running down the street that led to her house, tears stinging her eyes as she raced to the only place of safety she knew.

As the girl rushed through the door of her home she fled straight back to the room she shared with her sister and flung herself on their pink princess canopy bed. Her tears couldn't be held back and she wept for nearly an hour, her face buried in a ruffled pillow. Navi didn't fully comprehend where all of these tears were coming from but she knew they were bigger than her and there was nothing she could do to stop them.

By the time Thursday afternoon rolled around Navi was a nervous wreck. She had been pining for the chance to talk with the dance team leader but had not found an opportunity to connect with her. She was also doing all she could to keep things at home calm and quiet and had been sure not to let on about the encounter she had with the police officers. She truly did not understand the complexity of the situation but she knew nothing good would come from her discussing it with the mom or Mr. Earl.

As school let out Navi joined the rest of the dance team in the locker room. Spirits were high and the girls were all giggling and glowing in anticipation of the evening's performance. This was such a pure time of friendship and community for Navi and was unlike any experience she'd ever had. Finally accepted in the clique, she helped girls with their makeup and they helped her fix her hair. It seemed as if she was finally truly one of the team.

The crew left the junior high school and walked together down to the football stadium on the opposite end of the campus. As the early evening twilight started to fall the streetlights along the route began to glow and a cool autumn breeze blew against the pre-teens already rouged cheeks. The girls chattered away as they walked, talking about the routine, about boys, about pop stars and their current favorite songs. Navi was so delighted to just have the approval and get to hang out with these "cool" girls and she was cherishing each moment.

The dance team gathered in the locker room at the stadium and changed into their uniforms. There was a level of anticipation in the air that was absolutely electric. As the sky grew darker the fans started to gather in the stands. The game started and Navi knew Mr. Earl and her little sister were a part of the crowd tonight because they had promised they would be there to see her preform.

As the dance team took their place on the sidelines next to the cheerleaders they stretched and primped, preparing for their big show. The minutes of the game dissolved and as the halfway mark grew closer the dance coach gathered her team for one last pep talk. After the rally she pulled Navi aside.

"Navi, I don't know why you are even dressed and on

the field, you know the rules and skipping out on Tuesday's final practice means you are disqualified from the show this evening," the coach said firmly, her eyes glaring sharply at Navi.

"But, Coach! I have been practicing every day and I know the routine! I didn't skip on Tuesday, I had to leave and couldn't get back in time! It wasn't my fault!" the girl protested as her face turned red and her eyes filled with tears.

"I don't want to hear your excuses, and I don't want this behavior infecting the rest of the team. You get back in the locker room and remove that uniform immediately. I want you in street clothes and in the stands before my dance team takes the field for the halftime show," the coach hissed.

Navi felt as if she'd been punched in the stomach and there was no way she could hold back her tears. They began pouring from her swollen eyes as she turned and ran away from the sidelines and ducked into the locker room. Completely distraught, she tore off her uniform and put her school clothes back on. Wiping the tears from her face, she left the locker room and kept right on walking through the stadium gates. As she made her way down the sidewalk she heard the halftime song start and she counted off in her head, "Five, six, seven, eight..."

Navi cried as she walked home under the glow of the streetlights. She had never felt more alone. She realized that she had the mom and Mr. Earl and her little sister at home, but she didn't really feel like she was truly connected with any of them. There were lots of men and other girls like her who she often interacted with when they made movies or went to parties but she really didn't feel like there was an authentic connection with any of them, either. She had been led to believe that the dance team was finally the group where she would fit in, but obviously that was not her place either.

The tears falling down her cheeks seemed to be in time with her footsteps as she walked on. Suddenly there were footsteps alongside her, matching her pace.

"Hello, Navi," said the sweet, deep voice of the Father. "You are not alone."

"Father, I am so glad You are here, but I am alone!" Navi replied through her sobs. "I don't have anyone who loves me at home, the people who I see when we go to the parties and clubs aren't really my friends. Now I'm not even on the dance team anymore," she cried.

"Navi, I have been with you every moment, even when you were not aware I was there. I will never leave. I'm with you always, child," He reassured her. "You have made me proud as I've watched you be so brave. No matter what has happened you've always remained courageous and strong. My heart is filled with joy watching you grow and flourish."

These words caused Navi's tears to quickly dry up and disappear. She always felt such joy when the Father spoke over her and an unmistakable hope would start bubbling up inside of her. As she turned to walk down her street and the Father kept pace with her He had another bit of encouragement.

"Navi, you have come through so much and done so well, but now is the time for your resolve to truly be tested. Because of the plans I have for you and all those whose lives you will impact, this next season is going to be a time of stretching and testing, but always remember I am with you and I will never, ever leave you. I know you will make it through and I know the effect your life is going to make in the future. Be encouraged, child, and never, ever give up." He said as they reached her front door.

Navi pulled the key from under the mat and let herself in. As she sat quietly in the living room she reflected on her special time with the Father. This precious experience marked her deeply and the loneliness she had been feeling had completely melted away.

After a while Mr. Earl and her little sister came in and he was obviously very angry with Navi. He yelled at her for not participating in the halftime dance, he yelled at her for leaving without them and he yelled at her for not responding to his yelling. Navi just looked at his face and watched it turn redder and redder every time he raised his voice.

When Mr. Earl sent the little sister to bed for the night Navi went with her. Grabbing her arm as she made her way to the hallway, Mr. Earl reminded her he expected her to put the child to sleep and return to the living room for their special time together. Navi turned to look him square in the eye and flatly told him, "No."

She had no intention of joining him in the living room that evening and she was angry at him because she knew her missed opportunity with the dance team was a direct result of his actions, and that caused resentment to rise up inside of her.

Mr. Earl bristled against her rejection and gritted his teeth. He was displeased with the girl and made no effort to conceal his feelings. Letting go of her arm he grumbled as he turned back to the living room and let her go on into her bedroom.

That night Navi laid in the bed next to her little sister and did more thinking than sleeping. She thought about the dance team, about the police officers, about her walk with the Father. The words He had spoken over her gave her such hope, and when she finally did drift off to sleep her dreams were filled with faith and expectation.

[13]

BITTERSWEET JUSTICE

On Friday morning Navi woke up with a feeling of quiet confidence stirring inside of her. She quickly dressed and was headed to school before Mr. Earl or the mom had even made their coffee. Navi knew one of them would get her little sister to school and for some reason she was motivated to get out the door as quickly as possible this day.

When she got to the school she was surprised to see how many of her classmates arrived early for breakfast. She lived so close that she had never even considered having breakfast at the school, but since she was in the cafeteria and the sticky sweet smell of pancake syrup was swirling in the air, she happily got in line to pick out a little plastic tray of food. After digging out the cash she had been given to buy dinner at the game the night before she paid for her meal and looked around for a place to sit. Finding a table with a few familiar faces in the back of the room, she made her way to an empty seat.

The students at Navi's table were talking about the football game and their team's victory over the opponent. It sounded as if everything had gone well the night before and Navi was encouraged to hear the good report. Once breakfast was over they all parted ways before stopping by their lockers on their way to their homeroom classes. There was a simple purity to the camaraderie between the students and the early morning fellowship. This routine felt oddly familiar to Navi, even though it was a new experience for the girl.

Not long after the roll was called in the first class the all-to-familiar sound of the principal's office announcements came over the loudspeaker. When congratulations were made to the football team, coaches, cheerleaders and dance team for the great victory the night before it seemed as if the entire school broke into shouts and applause. The principal's assistant then went through the normal list of boring announcements including upcoming book fairs, field trips and football games, but before she hung up the microphone she ended her on air stint by once again calling Navi to the office.

After the shock of hearing her name called had melted away every bit of joy from that morning's adventures, Navi took a shaky, deep breath. The public shame and humiliation was nearly more than the young girl could bear as she stood up with her face beet red and exited the classroom amidst her fellow classmate's giggles and condescending remarks.

The walk to the principal's office was again filled with questions and wondering why, but once she opened the door to see the two policemen who had taken her downtown three days prior she no longer had to speculate.

The two men ushered her out the door and into the back of the waiting patrol car. As they drove to the station the gum snapper rattled off some things about Mr. Earl being arrested as they were leaving the school and how she should feel proud for being so brave. He promised her that she never had to worry about Mr. Earl trying to touch her privates again and that the police had done all they could to ensure her safety.

As they arrived downtown the officers took Navi back into the big room with all the desks and phones. The place was bustling with activity and people were milling around everywhere. She was informed that the interrogation room they had used last time was unavailable and she would have to sit by a desk until someone arrived to take her home. Navi could not understand why they had driven from downtown all the way to her school just so they could take her downtown to wait for someone to come pick her up, but instead of asking questions about their rationale she just sat quietly in the chair.

One of the officers brought her a soda and a bag of chips while she waited. She sipped and munched while she watched everything happening in that room. Navi was amazed at how these grown people were acting. Some of them smelled bad like they hadn't bathed in a long time and others were loud and obnoxious. Everyone but the police officers seemed to be out of control in one way or another and there was plenty of action to keep the girl distracted.

Suddenly, Navi heard a woman shouting loudly, "My baby! My baby!" When she turned to face the doorway she was absolutely shocked to see the mom running towards her, wailing shrilly.

"My poor baby! I can't believe he did this to you!" she cried as she dramatically fell in a pile in front of the desk. She heaved and sobbed there on the floor until two of the officers came to comfort her.

Navi couldn't wrap her brain around what was happening. The mom had never called her "my baby" and she had never witnessed her acting this way. She thought it seemed odd that she said something about 'not believing it had happened' because she had been there at the parties and the yacht clubs and the country clubs. Navi was sure the mom had watched the movies in their closet and saw the photos on Mr. Earl's desk.

She sat in the chair and watched the mom stand up with the help of an officer flanking each side. As the mom's wails became fewer and farther between, the gum snapping cop started slowly telling her some of the details of the case.

"Seems as if Mr. Earl and Mr. Smith may have attempted touching your daughter and one other student in her class," he smacked. "We've got her statement and Mr. Earl was taken into custody this morning. Someone from our office will be in touch with you next week to fill you in on the progress of the case. You just call us if you have any questions ma'am."

The mom batted her big blue eyes and nodded her head, panting from exhaustion after the grand emotional outburst. She gathered up her purse and had Navi come with her to the elevator. As they rode down to the parking garage the silence between them became as cold as steel. When they exited the elevator Navi followed the mom to the car and they each opened one of the front doors and sat down on the long bench seat.

They closed the doors in unison and Navi felt her skin crawl as the slamming sound echoed through the parking garage. It was a deeply surreal moment, almost like it was happening in a movie she was watching, but not in her reality.

"You little slut," the mom seethed through her clenched teeth. "I can't believe you couldn't keep your big mouth shut! It's bad enough you wouldn't keep your legs closed and stay away from MY man, but now you went and ran your mouth about it and ruined our lives. Do you even know what you've done you little tramp? We are about to lose everything! The cars, that house, the furniture, the clothes - all of it is about to be gone and it's all your fault! You're nothing but a worthless little whore!"

Navi could not understand what the mom was trying to say. Her head was spinning and her cheeks were getting hot. She could hear some of the words repeating over and over in her head:

"You little slut."

"We're about to lose everything."

"It's all your fault."

"You're nothing but a worthless little whore!"

The mom kept spouting out the slurs during the entire ride back to their suburban home. Navi didn't dare utter a word and she tightly held her tears in, staying silent and still in the passenger seat.

Once they returned home she attempted to bolt back to her bedroom and throw herself on the pink princess canopy bed, but the mom grabbed her by the arm and stopped her in the hallway.

"You better enjoy your perfect pink bedroom you little tramp! That will be the first thing to go and you'll see what happens after that. Everything in this house is about to disappear, all because you couldn't shut your fat mouth. This life wasn't free, honey - and now you're about to see what it really takes to survive!" she seethed at the child, her face just inches from Navi's.

Breaking free from the mom's grip, Navi escaped to her room and slammed the door. As soon as the door shut, a cascade of tears began to fall from her eyes and she couldn't hold back the flood of emotion any longer. Like black bricks piling up on her shoulders she allowed each of the words the mom had released over her begin to stack up until she was flattened under their weight. She laid facedown on the bed and cried in the pillow for what must have been hours, and only stopped when the mom opened the door to let two men come into the room.

"Navi, clean out those dresser drawers and take the blankets from that bed, these men are here to haul off this furniture," she said coldly.

The two men awkwardly came into the room and started unscrewing and dismantling the furniture while Navi did as she was instructed. Once she had the clothing and bedding stuffed into the closet she went out to the living room to get out of the way of the workers and to try and listen in on the phone calls the mom was making.

She heard the mom shouting into the phone about how unlawful the interview had been, about how many powerful people would be brought down by this, about how she was already doing what had to be done to scrape together the money. She heard the mom's angry voice groaning and yelling and cursing. When the phone was hung up and the mom came into the living room the men emerged from the bedroom, carrying parts of the bed outside to their waiting truck. After a few more trips toting off the mattress, mirror and dresser, they came back to stand at the front door as they counted several bills into the mom's open hand.

Closing the door as they left, she turned to look at Navi. There was a glare in her eyes that was unnatural and it intimidated the child. For the first time she realized Mr. Earl had acted as a buffer zone, as a layer of protection between her and the mom. And now he was gone.

"Navi, things are about to change around here in a very big way. Tomorrow morning some men are coming to haul off the furniture you're sitting on, and the television. We need to sell everything as quickly as possible to get together bail money and retain an attorney. I don't think you realize just how much Mr. Earl has done for us." The mom rattled off these statements to the girl and then walked into the bedroom she shared with Mr. Earl.

Navi stood in the doorway and watched the mom light one of her long, brown cigarettes before she picked up a box and started pulling the movies off the top shelf in the closet. Placing the tapes in the box two and three at a time, she worked her way around the big, walk-in closet and kept filling the box until they were all inside. Stamping out her cigarette in a crystal ashtray on the desk, she grabbed a fat roll of tape and secured the lid to the brown cardboard box.

As the mom started stuffing all of her dancing costumes and clothes into bags Navi's little sister came home from school. Sprinting to the door, the mom shoved Navi out of the way as she dashed past her to sweep up her little sister in her arms. She told her how she loved her and that everything would be okay through chokes of sobs and buckets of tears.

The little sister wasn't sure what to think and sweetly touched the mom's face. "Don't worry mamma, don't cry," she said innocently.

Confused by what was happening, she looked around the room to see Navi standing in the shadow of the hallway, head down and eyes swollen from crying most of the day. She would soon go to their bedroom to find the furniture gone and their belongings all stuffed in the closet.

The little sister had no idea what was going on and neither she nor Navi would ever be able to predict what the next few weeks of their life would hold.

[14]

RUN!

THE MOM WAS RIGHT ABOUT SO MANY THINGS. IT HAD been Mr. Earl who kept them in their nice suburban home. He had been the one who made sure they had food and nice clothes and new cars. The furniture, the decorations, all the things that made life comfortable were because of his income, his connections and his position. On the surface it had looked like they had everything they ever could ever need or want, but once he was removed from the picture that image quickly started crumbling away.

Because so much of what they had was on loan or had been traded to Mr. Earl for favors, once he was arrested items started disappearing. The bank came and took the cars, which never really belonged to them anyway. The living room furniture left the house much in the same way the girls' pink princess canopy bedroom set had went out the door. The televisions, art off the walls, some of the mom's nicer clothing - everything had a price and it was all either being repossessed or sold for cash to scrape together bail money and the lawyer's retainer.

During this time Navi was avoiding school as much as possible. Her few trips to her classes had ended with her rushing home in tears after some girls cornered her in the bathroom or locker room and called her names and teased her because she had kissed Mr. Earl. One afternoon she went to check her locker between classes and found that it had been stuffed with what seemed like hundreds of slips of paper with nasty words like tramp and slut written on each one. Navi didn't know how her classmates had gotten into her locker but she was so humiliated as the papers poured out when she opened the door all she could do was stand there and cry as a crowd gathered around her, laughing hysterically.

As much as Navi wanted to avoid school, she wanted to avoid home even more. The mom seemed to drink much more than she had before and when she was there the atmosphere was volatile. Sometimes she had people come to talk with Navi or took her somewhere where a stranger would interview her. In just a matter of weeks the girl had spoken with a caseworker, a psychiatrist, two attorneys, a mental health care worker and someone from a drug addiction rehabilitation center.

The mom always made sure to start every meeting by

telling the other adult that Navi had a long history of lying, that she had been smoking marijuana and having neighborhood boys put their hands up her shirt behind the local store and that her real dad had been schizophrenic and committed suicide. For all she knew the girl was already sleeping around with multiple boys, the mom would say.

Most of the interviews were all about Navi and how or what she thought or felt. If they asked if she was angry or hurt she usually would say yes, that she was angry at her mom for making her talk to whoever was questioning her. That yes, she was hurt by the kids at school calling her a tramp and a whore. They asked her about skipping school, which she was doing a lot of lately, and they would ask her about drinking alcohol and smoking pot, which she was doing more often than ever before.

The affirmative answers about smoking pot and drinking were especially concerning to the drug and alcohol counselor and Navi ended up locked up in the rehab center for 30 days. She quickly learned what a real drug addict was from the people she met there and made friends with some of the older teenagers who had already been using hard drugs like heroin and cocaine. When they told her what the high they experienced felt like she could hardly wait to try them. One of her new friends managed to sneak some LSD into the facility and he and Navi stayed up all night sneaking through the halls and hiding out in the kitchen as they tripped on the acid.

When she was finally released from drug rehab she was given a notice that a judge had declared her an unruly child and ordered her to attend 90 meetings for alcoholics and drug addicts within the next 90 days, so Navi knew she would be very busy over the next three months. It had been about six weeks since Mr. Earl had been arrested but so much had happened since that day it seemed like it had been forever.

While Navi was in the rehab the mom and her sister had packed what was left of their belongings and moved across town to a tiny, dilapidated clapboard house right off the freeway. And, since the mom had bailed him out of jail, Mr. Earl was there waiting for her when she came home. She walked in the doorway of the unfamiliar house and saw him sitting on the couch, a smug smile painted on his face. Totally shocked, she dropped the backpack of clothes and paperwork she had brought home from the treatment center on the floor by her feet and spun around to look at the mom as if to question his presence.

"Navi, I think you owe this man an apology! You could have ruined his career, and you nearly damaged his reputation in the city! He has done so much for us and your big mouth has nearly driven him away. Now you go over there and ask forgiveness for the hell you've brought into his life," the mom spat.

Navi was absolutely shocked! She didn't know what to think or how to react to this unbelievable situation, but she knew she would never be the one apologizing to this man. Her heart started beating a mile a minute and her face got red hot. The mom stood between Navi and the doorway, her hands on her hips and a toe tap-tap-tapping the ground as if to hurry the girl up.

Mr. Earl sat there with an arrogant smirk drawn across his face. Navi could literally feel every time he had ever touched her, every time he had kissed her, every time he had laid on top of her, his head turned slightly, his teeth and eyes clenched in ecstasy. She was standing before him, reliving each experience in a moment. Her heart pounded so hard she thought it would burst out of her chest and explode.

"No!" the girl shouted as she scooped up her little backpack and ran right past the giant of a mom, out the door and into the unfamiliar streets of the new neighborhood.

Navi had no plans of what direction to go, she just wanted to escape the situation she had been put in and get as far away from the mom and Mr. Earl as she could. She ran towards the noisy highway and cut left down the service road. Noticing the ledge at the top of the underpass that made a bridge under the freeway she bolted up the concrete ramp to hide. She had a great vantage point and from there she could watch for the mom coming after her and see people coming and going from the small convenience store on the corner.

Navi stooped down in the ledge under that bridge for

a long time and she never saw the mom come by to try and find her. As the minutes turned to hours and the sun started going down she had stretched out and dug a sweatshirt from her backpack. Once night had fallen she used the backpack like a little pillow and allowed herself to doze off a few times. It was noisy under the bridge as cars zoomed overtop of her, and there were some rodents and bats that had made their homes in that space, so the sounds of their scurrying made it hard for Navi to truly find rest.

As the rising sun cast everything an amber glow the next morning Navi stretched out in her cramped quarters, giving up her quest for sleep. Because her stomach was growling and she was so thirsty, she decided to go down into the little store and try to get something to fill her empty belly with. Gathering her backpack she made the short trek down to the rickety little shop.

When she came in the door she could feel the old man who worked the counter watching her like a hawk. She hoped he would be distracted by a customer paying for their items and when one of them had his attention she saw her chance and slipped a bag of chips into her backpack. Navi had never stolen anything before and she was terrified of being caught this time, so she quickly turned around to get out of the store as fast as possible.

Trying to cut down the aisle closest to the door, she was abruptly stopped by the shopkeeper. He had a twisted smile on his face as he stood between the girl and the doorway, blocking her escape.

"Did you want to pay for that bag of chips little girl?" he asked, his gnarled smile revealing missing teeth and black gums.

Navi's head dropped. "I don't have any money," she stammered.

"Well, I'll tell ya what, young lady, if you want I'll let you pay with a yankee dime, what do you say about that? And you can get anything else you want too, how does that sound?" the man smiled.

Navi wasn't sure what he meant by a yankee dime, but she understood she wouldn't have to pay, which was a huge relief. She grabbed a sandwich and a candy bar asking, "Can I have these for one of those yankee dimes too?" a glimmer coming across her young eyes.

"Sure honey, help yourself to anything you want. Get a soda pop too, or would a girl like you rather have a can of beer?" he asked with a chuckle.

The thought of drinking a sour beer didn't appeal much to Navi but she knew the alcohol would give her anxious body that calm, tingly feeling so she took the man up on his offer and grabbed one from the cooler. Once she had gathered all her supplies into her backpack he led her up to the counter.

Raising the divider to allow the girl to come back behind the register her waved her through a door into his tiny office. Giving her a boost he sat her up on the desk and made sure she had everything she had selected out in the storefront. Navi was so happy to have food and drink and be in a nice, warm place to eat. The man seemed pretty happy about the situation as well, but before the girl could open her bag of chips he grabbed her hand and said, "Wait a minute honey, you haven't paid for those yet."

"Oh yeah," replied Navi, "you wanted me to pay with play money. Here's your dime mister," she joked as she pretended to drop an invisible coin into his hand.

"Oh no, no, my little friend. That's not a yankee dime, this is," he said slyly, leaning towards her and giving her a gruesome kiss as his hand went up the front of her shirt.

Navi was paralyzed and sat on the desk frozen in time, the crumpled bag of chips still in her hand. She could feel the old man's sticky tongue trying to poke itself between her lips as he panted against her face. He was pressing his body against her tiny frame while his gruff hands groped whatever they could find to grab. Navi could feel her heart pounding in her throat but she was so helpless she couldn't cry out or push the man away.

The chimes of the door opening and a customer coming into the store were the only thing that stopped the man's advances. He left Navi sitting up on the desk to go out and ring the order and as soon as she saw her chance she slung her bag over her shoulder and bolted past the counter, right out the door.

Navi ran.

She ran down the street as fast as she could go and took the first opportunity to cut left up a side street. She kept on running, not knowing if the old man was chasing her but certain she was able to outsmart him if she couldn't outrun him. The girl didn't have a plan of where she was running to and didn't have anywhere to go. She couldn't go home, she couldn't go to the school or to the police, she couldn't go to her grandmom or to anyone else. No one had ever tried to help her and no one had ever tried to stop Mr. Earl and his friends.

Suddenly she realized she wasn't just running from the shopkeeper anymore, but she was running from everything. She was running from the mom, from Mr. Earl, from the girls in the locker room, from the police officers, from the judge, from the workers at the rehab clinic. She was running from every man who had ever touched her and every photo or video that had ever been made of her or shown to her.

Navi finally stopped running when she made it to an abandoned softball field. She found her way to the old rundown dugout and ducked inside, hidden behind the walls that seemed to be held together by faded blue paint. When she plopped down on the bench, gasping to catch her breath, she realized there was something she had not meant to run from but she had unintentionally left behind. As her mind stopped racing her heart began to ache as she thought of how she had left her little sister alone. She hadn't even said goodbye. Suddenly the girl was overcome with fear that Mr Earl and his friends would try to do the things they had done to her as well.

"Navi, do not be afraid. I am with you and I am with your sister also," she heard the deep, rich voice of the Father say. As His presence drew near to her the fear was driven away.

"Father, I have been through so much trouble and pain, I don't know if I can take anymore. And I never want my little sister to have to go through any of this," Navi sobbed as she buried her face in His warm chest. She poured her heart out to Him and cried and cried and cried. As she wept she told Him about all the things that she had been through and all the things she had seen. She just kept crying until all her tears were used up and she felt completely spent.

"Navi, I was there with you through it all. I saw everything and I wept bitterly as I watched those men go farther and farther from Me and farther and farther from fulfilling the purpose I placed them on this earth for. But I always knew you would be with Me, Navi. I know you will never separate yourself from Me," He said. "Put Me in your heart and take Me with you, child. I will never leave you or forsake you."

"Father, I want You in my heart," the girl said, now down on the ground with her knees in the dirt and her elbows propped up on the bench as if she were praying at the altar of a church. "Please don't ever leave me, please be with me forever," she pled.

The Father pulled His robe over her and covered her tiny body with the heavy cloak. "Child, you never have to beg Me, it is my pleasure to remain in you and with you," He answered.

Navi climbed up on the bench and stretched out to rest her head upon His lap. She fell asleep there with His robe covering her like a blanket and she slept through the night with dreams filled with revelations of her purpose and destiny running through her mind.

When Navi woke the next morning she felt rested and peaceful at first. She remembered the special time she had spent with the Father and the kind words He had spoken over her. She thought of her dreams and her destiny. She thought of the warmth she had felt fill her whole body when she had asked Him to make a home inside of her heart.

But that warm feeling seemed to fade as she thought of her little sister being left behind with Mr. Earl. It was as if she could hear a voice telling her that if anything happened to that child it would be all her fault. The more she paid attention to that voice the louder it grew and the less she felt the warmth of the Father. Navi remembered the can of beer she had stuffed in her bag and she pulled it out, hoping that guzzling down the sour drink would chase away the feelings of anxiety welling up within her.

The drink did help her to feel calmer, but it didn't seem like quite enough for her. She started to think about how her mind would be racing again once this drink wore off and she could almost hear a voice again telling her to go find more to be sure those feelings wouldn't come back.

Navi listened to that voice and picked up her backpack and walked down the streets she had been running on the day before. She knew she had slept for nearly an entire day in that baseball dugout because everything she saw was evidence of a new morning. Children were getting into big yellow busses and parents were backing out of driveways to head to work. Birds were flying around from telephone poles to treetops and people were walking out of fast food restaurants with brown bags of breakfasts in their hands.

Once Navi made it to the highway she walked along the feeder road with no intention of going anywhere particular but a strong desire to get as far away from where she was as possible. As she stepped one foot in front of the other she was surprised when a car pulled off the road in front of her. The passenger window came down and a cute girl probably not too much older than Navi waved her over. When Navi got close enough to see inside the vehicle she realized an attractive older boy was driving and another pretty teenager was in the backseat.

"Hey girl, you want a ride?" the passenger asked her. Navi knew better than to ride with strangers so she was a little apprehensive to even respond to the question.

The girl in the backseat spoke up asking, "Do you want more than a ride? You wanna get high?" she smiled, pulling a bag of pot out of her pocket to show Navi.

That was all it seemed to take and Navi happily agreed to get in the car, climbing in the backseat with her new found friend. She had no idea who these people were and no idea where they may be headed, but she knew those tormenting voices, thoughts and memories wouldn't be able to harass her as long as she stayed high. As the driver pulled up onto the freeway the girl in the backseat started stuffing a glass pipe with the weed from her sack and the girl in the front turned around and smiled at Navi.

"We're headed to Tennessee. We've got a friend there we can all stay with and he said he knows how we can get jobs and make some money," she said, jerking her thumb at the driver.

"I never said I was gonna get us jobs, I said I knew how we can make some money," the driver replied with a laugh.

"Whatever," the girl responded, rolling her eyes. Directing her attention back to Navi she asked, "Do you wanna go all the way with us? We've got enough gas and enough weed to get there," she chuckled.

"Sure," Navi answered. "I don't have anywhere else I can go."

She took the glass pipe being handed to her and let her new friend light it up. Taking three long puffs from it she immediately felt her whole body relax as she released the smoke in the confines of the little car.

"Ah, that feels much better," she smiled, melting back into the seat and gazing out the window as cars and buildings sped by. They drove on through the town, passing the pipe around and filling the car with smoke as they trekked onward. Once they were on the open highway outside of the city the driver cranked up the volume on the radio and cracked open the windows to let some of the pungent smoke out. The foursome laughed and sang, talking and joking and smoking as the miles passed and the minutes melted into hours.

Navi didn't know how far away Tennessee was but she was just relieved to be putting distance between herself and the mom and Mr. Earl. Despite her hazy high she knew the Father was with her, because that warm feeling that overtook her when she invited Him into her heart was still radiating within her.

All of the destiny dreams He had released over her were hidden deep down inside of her and she somehow knew that no matter what happened, she would ultimately be with Him again.

AFTERWORD

Navi's story is not over, it merely began on these pages. To learn where she ended up from here and read about what happened next, get the other two books in this series: *Hello Navi* & *Goodbye Navi*.

Find ordering info at authorsandystorm.com and footprintpub.com.

ABOUT THE ARTIST

Alexis Kadonsky is a fine artist, 3D animator, and designer from Chicagoland, born in 1990.

On a fully funded art scholarship, Alexis received a BFA in graphic design from the University of Illinois Ubana-Champaign. She continued on to achieve her MFA in 3D Computer Animation from the School of Visual Arts in New York City and was named Sony Pictures Imageworks IPAX Scoredos Scholar for exemplary achievements and truly special talent and passion for film, effects, and animation.

Alexis embraces her attention to detail throughout many mediums as demonstrated in her diverse portfolio. Art acts as an escape for Alexis, and she strives to tell a unique story with her work while enjoying getting lost in the process of creating. She also has a passion for travel and has spent about two years of her life traveling around Europe and Australia to further expand her views on art and the world. Although her work is inspired from many paths, Alexis believes her best creativity ignites from her personal experiences.

See more of Alexis Kadonsky's work at www.alexiskadonsky.com.

ABOUT ANIMALS AT SUNDOWN

A child writing a poem like this should alert adults that there is something scary and traumatic happening. I wrote this poem at just 11 years old and was so proud that I shared it with anyone who would give me the time of day. Even my mother and some of the men who came to our house had read the poem, but no one heard my plea.

As the trusted adult in a child or teenager's life, it is up to us to listen carefully for cries for help. Learn more about signs of sexual abuse and trafficking and quickly report any suspicions to law enforcement immediately. Visit authorsandystorm.com for some easy tools to use with kids and teens to start having these crucial conversations.

When Alexis and I discussed the images to use for this poem, I asked her to create animals that looked like wild predators and conveyed emotions of fear - like the fear I felt nearly every night of my childhood.

Once again, this brilliant artist created images that far surpassed even my wildest imaginations.

Animals At Sundown

Some lay their sleepy heads,
At this time of day;
Others awaken as the cool breezes blow;
Ready to hunt, WILDLY

Some rest, lay and sleep.
Others stretch, awaken and stir;
Ready to KILL for food.

Some hide, afraid, alone and scared
Others attack and search slyly;
Ready to spring on anything around.

Some hide, terrified the OTHERS
will find them.

Sandy Storm, 11 years old

ABOUT THE AUTHOR

"If anyone belongs to Christ, there is a new creation.
The old things have gone; everything is made new!"
                                        - 2 Corinthians 5:17 NCV

Author Sandy Storm is a child sex trafficking survivor who has experienced a powerful transformation and lives what can only be described as a brand new life.

She is an author and gifted public speaker, communicating her experiences while trapped as a child sex slave and involved in the industry of commercial sexual exploitation as a young adult as well as the effects of porn on our culture and the need for care for child sex trafficking survivors.

Generously gifted with a creative spirit, Sandy is an inspiration to many. She shares her story of great love, hope, forgiveness and redemption as she speaks and teaches through many avenues within the church and the marketplace.

Her presentations have been called educational,

inspiring and powerful and attendees say they leave feeling empowered to bring positive change to their circles of influence.

Sandy has been married to her amazing husband since 2003 and they are involved in their communities through their businesses and the local church.

Learn more about ways you can help to bring an end to human trafficking and the industry of commercial sexual exploitation at authorsandystorm.com.

Follow Sandy on social media and contact her at sandy@authorsandystorm.com.

f **O** @authorsandystorm

Sandy's life has been redeemed from victim to survivor, and now she is truly thriving.

Photo by Fallon Michael